Julie
1974

The Big Break

by Megan McDonald

★ American Girl®

A Peek into
Julie's World

Julie lives in an apartment right above her mother's second-hand shop, Gladrags. If her mom needs her help in the shop, Julie just pops downstairs.

Julie's Family and Friends

Mom
Julie's mother,
who runs a store

Dad
Julie's father,
a pilot

Tracy
Julie's sister,
who is 15

Ivy
Julie's best friend,
who is 9

T. J.
A boy at school
who plays basketball

Coach Manley
A gym teacher and
basketball coach

Table of Contents

Moving Day

✿ **Chapter 1** ✿

The world spun—first upside down, then right-side up again—as Julie Albright and her best friend, Ivy Ling, turned cartwheels around the backyard.

"Watch me do a backflip!" called Ivy.

She leaned back, stretching her neck like a tree bending in the wind. Soon her shiny black ponytail bounced upside down as she twirled through the air, landing perfectly on two feet.

"I always fall flat on my face!" said Julie. "I'll never be as good as you, no matter how hard I practice." She sighed. "I'm sure going to miss doing gymnastics with you after school every day."

"I'm going to miss playing basketball in your driveway," said Ivy, "even though you always beat me."

Julie stuck out her lower lip and made an exaggerated sad face. Both girls fell down laughing. Then they stretched out on the grass, folding their hands behind their heads, and gazed dreamily at the clear blue sky, a perfect September day.

"Hey, look," said Julie, pointing to an airplane high up

in the sky. "Maybe that's my dad! Hi, Dad!" The two girls whooped and yelled and waved.

Mr. Albright was a pilot. Julie always waved at every airplane she saw, imagining it might be her dad flying to some exotic, far-off country.

"What are you going to miss most?" Julie asked.

"Walking to school together and sitting behind you in class," said Ivy.

"Who am I going to be lunch buddies with?" said Julie. "You're the only friend in the world who would trade me your Twinkie for a pickle!"

"Julie!" Mom called from the back porch as she took down some hanging geraniums. "Time to get a move on. The van will be here in half an hour."

"I guess I had better get going," said Ivy.

"Not yet!" said Julie. "Come up to my room with me while I make sure I'm all packed."

Upstairs, Julie scooped up Nutmeg, her pet rabbit, from her favorite spot in the laundry basket and plopped down cross-legged next to Ivy on her bed. Ivy stroked Nutmeg's velvet-brown fur, while Julie scratched her pet behind her floppy lop ears. "I'm sure gonna miss you, girl," said Julie, kissing Nutmeg on her wiggly nose and nuzzling her whiskers. "But Ivy's going to take extra-special good care of you whenever Dad's gone."

Julie took a long last look around her room. Ghosts of posters that had once decorated the walls formed an empty gallery around the room, showing off the flowered wallpaper. Craters in the blue shag rug made a strange moonscape, a map of where Julie's desk and dresser had once been. Boxes were piled everywhere. The room was middle-of-the-night quiet.

"I still can't believe you're moving," said Ivy, flashing her dark eyes at Julie.

"It's only a few miles away, across town," said Julie. "It's not like I'm moving to Mars."

"I won't be able to blink lights at you from across the street anymore to say good night," said Ivy.

"But we can call each other," Julie pointed out. "And you'll still see me on the weekends when I come visit my dad." There was that lump again. She felt it every time she thought of being without Dad. She thought she'd gotten used to the idea of her parents being divorced, but now that she wouldn't be living with Dad anymore, suddenly it wasn't just an idea. It was real.

"Here," said Julie. "I made us friendship bracelets. We can both wear them and think of each other." She handed a colorful knotted bracelet to Ivy.

"Neat!" said Ivy. "Here, tie it on my wrist."

Julie's big sister, Tracy, poked her head into Julie's room.

"Mom says to start bringing our stuff down. Set it in the front room."

"Not yet!" Julie protested. "Just a few more minutes." It was bad enough they were making her move. Now they were taking away her last moments with her best friend, too.

"Mom says *now*," said Tracy, sounding annoyed.

Julie got up and tried lifting a too-heavy box, then set it back down and began dragging a garbage bag across the floor instead. "Now I know why they call it Labor Day," she grumbled.

"I guess I better go, for real this time," said Ivy. Julie nodded. The two friends hooked pinkies in a secret handshake they'd had since kindergarten. Neither girl wanted to be the one to let go first.

A few hours later, Julie, Tracy, and Mom sat on the floor of their new apartment, holding cardboard cartons of Chinese takeout. Mom had pushed a few moving boxes together to serve as a table, and their dinner was spread out on top of the boxes.

"It's so great here," said Tracy. She paused to slurp some noodles off her chopsticks. "You should see all the groovy shops I passed along Haight Street when I went to get the takeout!"

Julie admired the way her big sister was always so

confident about everything. She wished she could be certain she'd like it here.

"My favorite part is that we live above my shop now," said Mom. "Think of it! To go to work, I just have to run downstairs!"

A few months ago, Mom had opened a shop on the corner of Redbud and Frederick. The shop was called Gladrags, and it was full of handmade stuff, such as purses made of worn-out blue jeans. Mom had told Julie the name was from the Rod Stewart song that went *"the handbags and the gladrags . . ."* The name was Tracy's idea. She had heard the song on the radio.

"How about you, Julie?" asked Mom. "What do you think you're going to like best about living here?"

Julie glanced around the room. Tiny rainbows of color danced across the empty walls, flashing from the prism Mom had hung in the front window.

"Well, um, I especially like the dining table," Julie decided, pointing to the boxes they were eating on. Mom and Tracy laughed.

"The real dining table isn't put back together yet," said Mom. "I couldn't find the screwdriver."

The doorbell rang, and Tracy ran to answer it. "Mom, it's some guy," she announced.

Julie looked up from her chicken chow mein. Standing in the doorway was a curious-looking man. He had a bushy red beard and wiry red hair, and he wore a patched green army jacket and a baseball cap.

"Hank!" said Mom, standing up. "C'mon in. Girls, this is Hank, a friend from the neighborhood. He was my first customer the day I opened the shop!"

"Far out," said Tracy.

"Hank, these are my girls, Tracy and Julie."

"I've heard a lot about you from your mom," said Hank. "Here." He held out a plate covered with foil. "I brought some of my famous zucchini bread to welcome you to the neighborhood."

"Yum!" said Julie, peering under the aluminum foil.

"Thanks," said Mom, taking the plate of zucchini bread. "Can't wait to taste it. Can you stay for some tea?"

"No, I'm on my way to a big meeting about the Vet Center. But thank you." He tipped his cap at Julie and Tracy, and left.

"That was so nice of him," said Tracy.

Mom nodded. "Hank's a good egg." She set the plate on the kitchen counter. "Now, where were we?"

"I'll help you put together the dining table if you'll help

me fix up my room," said Julie. "I need curtains. And a shade for my lamp."

"We can make curtains," said Mom. "And decorate a lampshade. Hey, how would you like one of those fuzzy rugs in the shape of a foot?"

"Okay," said Julie, helping Mom clear away the leftovers.

"I volunteer to wash the dishes tonight!" said Tracy.

"There aren't any dishes," said Julie. "We ate out of the boxes."

"Exactly!" Tracy grinned. She pretended to practice tennis against the living-room wall with an imaginary racket—first her forehand, then her backhand. "I just can't wait for school. I'm going out for the tennis team. Maybe debate, too. But definitely tennis," Tracy chattered on. "Someday I want to go to France. To the French Open."

"What's that?" Julie asked.

"It's only a world-famous tennis match. Chrissie Evert won the Grand Slam there for the last two years in a row!"

"My sister's a tennis freak," Julie announced.

Tracy pretended to lob the ball right at her sister. "Fifteen–love!" said Tracy.

"I don't see how I'm going to start a new school this week," Julie said when Mom came to tuck her in. "I don't even know where a pencil is, or my binder or anything.

What if I left some of the stuff I need at Dad's? What if I get lost trying to find my classroom? What if nobody talks to me and I can't find a friend?"

"Honey, I know this is all new, and it's not going to be easy at first," Mom said, sitting down beside Julie on the bed. "But I'll take you the first day, and we'll meet your teacher and make sure you know your way around. And how could the other kids not like you?" Mom reached to hug her.

Julie squirmed away. "You don't understand."

"Look, I know starting over in a new place is scary. It's scary for me, too, starting a new business. But sometimes you just have to trust in yourself and take a chance." Mom kissed Julie on the top of her head and turned out the light.

A New School

❀ **Chapter 2** ❀

On the first day of school at Jack London Elementary, Julie's teacher wrote her name in perfect cursive on the board: Ms. Hunter.

"You forgot the 'r' in Mrs.," a boy in the back row pointed out.

"It's *Ms.* Hunter," she told the class, drawing out the word "mizzz" to sound like a buzzing bee. "Not Miss or Mrs."

"Huh?" The students looked at each other, confused.

"Think of it like Mr. You call a man Mr. whether he's married or not, right?" The class nodded silently. "Well, Ms. is the same thing, for a woman."

"But why?" asked a bold girl named Alison. "What's wrong with Miss or Mrs.?"

"Whether or not a woman is married is her private business," Ms. Hunter explained. "Ms. works either way."

Julie carefully wrote out "Ms. Hunter" in her best cursive. She wasn't sure she understood. Would people be calling her mother Ms. Albright now?

The only kid who talked to Julie all day was the boy

who sat next to her in class. He had a short mop of sandy hair, a spray of freckles across his nose, and a funny name that sounded like a president. Every time Ms. Hunter called him Thomas Jefferson, Julie had to hold back a giggle. "It's T. J.," the boy corrected her.

When Ms. Hunter told the class to take out their rulers, Julie didn't have one. The girls behind her whispered and twittered. Julie heard the scornful words "new girl" and "divorced." She instantly felt her cheeks get hot. How in the world could they know about that already?

"Don't mind them," whispered T. J. "Amanda, Alison, and Angela. To get into their club, your name has to start with an A."

Julie nodded. The Water Fountain Girls. She'd seen them hanging around the water fountain that morning, pointing and snickering.

T. J. handed Julie a ruler. "Here, you can borrow mine. I have an extra."

"Thanks," said Julie. "We just moved, and it's kind of hard to find stuff in all the boxes."

Before T. J. could reply, Ms. Hunter broke in. "Julie Albright. In my class, we don't speak when the teacher is talking."

"But I didn't have a—"

"It's okay this time," said Ms. Hunter. "But remember,

boys and girls. Any talking out of turn is a demerit."

Great, thought Julie. *First day of school and I'm already in trouble.*

Julie found herself looking over her shoulder whenever she left her classroom. Principal Sanchez was all rules and no nonsense. He pointed with a pencil and warned kids to slow down or lower their voices. "Young man, tuck in your shirt!" he told a third-grader. "I hope that's not gum you're chewing," he scowled at another student. "One more warning and you'll get a demerit." Julie soon knew all about Mr. Sanchez's demerit system. Three demerits and you had to stay after school to wash blackboards.

At the end of the day, after the school bell had rung, Julie lingered at her locker. She was in no hurry to get home to an empty apartment. Julie pulled the most recent postcard from Dad out of her book bag and taped it to the inside of her locker door. Just as she slammed her locker shut and started down the hallway, a ball bounced into the hall through the open doors that led to the playground. The ball bounced against the lockers and rolled down the hall, right past her feet. A basketball!

Julie scooped it up and dribbled down the hallway to

"I used to play a lot with my dad," Julie told him.

the doors, glancing over her shoulder to make sure that Principal Sanchez was not nearby. On the playground, a few boys were horsing around near the far basketball hoop, playing what looked more like dodgeball than basketball. Out of the corner of her eye, Julie saw T. J. bending down, tying his sneaker.

"Think fast!" she called, tossing the ball at T. J. He jumped up, caught the ball in midair, and then drove toward the basket. Julie threw down her book bag and followed him down the court.

"Bet you can't get the ball back," T. J. teased, switching from right to left, bouncing the ball back and forth, light on his feet. Quick as a cat, Julie crouched low, sprang forward, and with one clean swipe, snatched the ball away from T. J.

"Good steal," T. J. said as Julie dribbled around him. "You shoot hoops?"

Julie did a layup and dribbled back over to T. J. "I used to play a lot with my dad," she told him.

"Hey, how are you at jump shots?" T. J. asked. "Will you try blocking me on my jump shots so I can practice? I want to play on the school team."

"There's a basketball team here?" asked Julie.

"Yeah. Fourth-, fifth-, and sixth-graders can join," said T. J. "We get to play against other schools. Mr. Manley's the coach. He posts a sign-up sheet outside his office."

T. J. turned and dribbled hard to the left, but Julie stuck to him like glue. For the next ten minutes, they took turns practicing and defending jump shots, layups, and rebounds.

"Hey, that was boss! Wanna help me again tomorrow?" T. J. asked. "Same time, same place?"

"Really? Sure! That'd be great," Julie told him.

And for the first time since the move, she found herself looking forward to tomorrow.

All week, Julie practiced after school with T. J. Now she'd be able to surprise Dad with some new moves on Saturday. She could hardly wait. Two whole days to see Ivy, play with Nutmeg, hang out with Dad, and sleep in her own room again. It would be just like old times.

First thing Saturday morning, Julie packed her paisley suitcase and waited by the door for Dad to arrive. Tracy came out in her pj's, rubbing her eyes as if she had just awakened.

"You better hurry up!" Julie said. "You're not even dressed. Dad's going to be here any minute, and he doesn't like to have to wait."

"I'm not going," said Tracy.

"What do you mean you're not going? It's Saturday. It's our day to go to Dad's and spend the weekend with him."

"Well, I'm staying here. I have tennis practice anyway,

and a bunch of us might go see a movie tonight."

"What about Dad? You can't decide not to go, just like that." Julie snapped her fingers. "We're still a family, you know, and Dad's part of it, too."

Tracy shook her head. "Give it up, Julie. We're never going to be a regular family again. This isn't *The Brady Bunch*. Besides, I'm in high school now. I'm old enough to decide for myself what I do on the weekends."

"You think you're so . . ." Julie hesitated but couldn't find the right words.

Toot, toot. Dad had said he'd honk for them so he wouldn't have to find a parking place. "He's here!" said Julie. "What am I supposed to tell him?"

"Whatever you want," said Tracy. "I don't care."

Toot, toot, toot. Dad was waiting.

"So you won't care if I tell him my sister turned into an *alien*?" Julie grabbed her suitcase, ran down the back stairs, kissed her mom good-bye in the shop, and rushed out to the waiting car.

"So, do you have everything?" asked Dad. "Where's your sister?"

"She's not coming." Julie looked down, absently rubbing at a scab on her arm.

"But it's our . . . never mind. Wait here. I'll be right back." Dad sprinted up the steps to the front door. Julie could see him gesturing with his hands as he talked with Tracy, who stood in her bathrobe with her arms crossed. Finally, Dad came back, without Tracy, and started the car.

He was extra quiet, so Julie tried to think of things to say. She chattered on about how all the kids were looking forward to their dads coming to Career Day at school on Monday. Julie decided to make the most of her weekend with Dad and forget about her crabby sister. Besides, she realized, it might be nice having Dad all to herself for a change.

As soon as they pulled up to the house, Ivy came running across the street. "Julie! You're here!"

"What do you say we head down to the Wharf?" asked Dad, pulling Julie's suitcase out of the trunk. "There's a festival at Ghirardelli Square today, with face painting, jugglers, magicians, and even a no-hands chocolate-eating contest!"

Julie and Ivy looked at each other with delight. "Can we ride the cable car?" Julie asked.

"Why not," said Dad.

Ivy ran back to her house to ask her parents for permission, and soon they were on their way.

Ding! Ding! rang the bell on the cable car. Julie and Ivy hopped up onto the open-air platform while Dad paid the fare. They gripped the poles tightly as the wind whipped their hair. Wheeee! The girls giggled with roller-coaster glee as the cable car barreled down the hill toward the waterfront.

They hopped off the cable car near Ghirardelli Square.

Music blared, kites fluttered, and a juggler on stilts amazed the crowd. Dad spread a blanket on the grass, and they had a picnic on the green, sipping hot chocolate as they watched a mime pretend to climb a flight of stairs.

"Guess what—I'm going to play basketball!" Julie announced. "Sign-up is next week."

"That's great, honey," Dad said. "It's nice to have a club to go to after school."

"It's not just a club, Dad. It's a real basketball team, with a coach and games against other schools and everything."

"I know you'll be a starter on the team," said Ivy. "You're so good at basketball."

"Wow," said Dad. "They have a girls' basketball team at your new school?"

"Not a girls' team. Just a team," said Julie.

"You're joining an all-boys' basketball team?" asked Ivy.

"Why not? T. J.'s my only friend at school, and he's going to play," said Julie. "He says I'm just as good as most of the boys."

Dad put his hand on Julie's shoulder. "Honey, I know you're good, but I've never heard of girls playing on the boys' team. It's a whole different thing playing on a team. It's not like shooting hoops with me in the driveway. A team can be a lot of pressure."

"It's not pressure to me," said Julie. "It's fun!"

"Well, boys can be super competitive at that age, and they like to roughhouse," Dad continued. "Did you ever think they might not be too happy about having a girl on their team? I'm not so sure it's a good idea, Julie. I don't want you getting hurt."

Julie rolled her eyes. "Da-ad, I'm not going to get hurt! In the newspaper, I saw this picture of a girl from Ohio who got to play on the boys' football team. And football's a lot rougher than basketball."

"Look, honey, I'm just not sure about this. Let me think about it. And I'll need to talk it over with your mother, too."

Once Julie saw the exclamation-point creases between Dad's eyebrows, she knew it was time to drop the subject.

That night, when Dad came to say good night, Julie asked him, "Dad, you're still coming to school on Monday, right? Like we planned?"

"Of course. It's World's Greatest Dad Day, right? And I'm supposed to wear my pajamas."

"No, Dad! It's Career Day, remember? The kids in my class think it's cool that you're a pilot. You have to wear your uniform!"

"Okay," said Dad. "I guess I won't wear my pajamas, then. Lights out, now. Good night, sleep tight."

"'Night, Dad." Julie waited for a moment and then said, "Dad, you forgot—"

"Don't let the bedbugs bite!" said Dad.

As soon as the lights were out, Julie saw a flash of light in her window coming from across the street. Ivy was signaling good night with their secret code.

Julie tiptoed across the room to the light switch. She blinked the light ten times in an on-off-on-off Morse code for *Good night, sleep tight, don't let the bedbugs bite!*

Career Day

❀ Chapter 3 ❀

On Monday morning, Julie watched the clock, waiting for social studies to be over. The rest of the day would be Career Day, when some of the fathers would come to tell the class about their jobs. Dad was going to share an exciting story about the time he had to make an emergency landing.

The first Career Day parent was Cathy's dad, a baker who went to work in the middle of the night. He brought cream-filled doughnuts for everybody. Kenneth's dad worked at a bank and gave each of the kids a newly minted penny. Robin's dad was a dentist. He gave out special tablets to chew that turned everyone's teeth pink in the places that needed to be brushed better.

Julie was only half listening. It would be Dad's turn any minute. Where was he? Dad was never late—

"Sorry I'm late!" a voice whispered in her ear. Not a Dad voice. *Mom!* What was she doing here? Then, in one heart-sinking moment, Julie knew. Mom had come to break the bad news to her—Dad couldn't be here today.

"Now, our last visitor is Mr. Albright, Julie's father,"

Ms. Hunter announced. "Mr. Albright is a pilot."

Julie slunk down lower in her chair as Mom made her way to the front, bracelets jangling, and whispered something to the teacher. Then Mom turned and faced the class.

"Hello, fourth grade! I'm Julie's mom, Mrs. Albright. As much as Julie's dad wanted to be here, he just couldn't be. He had to fill in for another pilot who was sick. Right now he's about twenty-seven thousand feet above the Rocky Mountains."

Oh no. This wasn't happening! Julie wanted to yell STOP, but she froze in her seat while the rest of the class began firing off questions.

"What kind of plane does he fly? Is it a 747?"

"Has he ever been to Hawaii?"

"Did he ever have to make a crash landing?"

"Why is your name Mrs. Albright if you're divorced?"

The room grew quiet. The question hung in the air like fog that wouldn't lift. Julie knew it had to be one of the Water Fountain Girls who had asked it, but she didn't dare turn her head. She stared at a pair of initials carved in her desktop as if it were a work of art in a museum.

"Class," said Ms. Hunter, "remember how we talked about not asking personal questions? Julie's mother has been kind enough to take the time to tell us about her career. So let's give her our full attention. There will be plenty of time for questions at the end."

How could this be happening? Julie had bragged to the whole class about the World's Greatest Pilot, her dad. Not her mom, the . . . junk-store lady!

Mom was already pulling a heap of junk out of her old tie-dyed bag. If only Julie could be like Samantha on *Bewitched,* her favorite TV show. One twitch of the nose and she'd blink herself right out of there in an instant. While she was at it, she would blink herself back to her old school. Her old *life.*

"Have you ever wondered," asked Mom, "what to do with old string? A pair of ripped-up jeans? Even apple seeds?"

No, thought Julie. *You throw them away in the garbage!*

Mom began passing around some of the handmade items she carried at the shop: denim purses, macramé plant hangers, and apple-seed bracelets. Julie looked at the clock. Wasn't that bell *ever* going to ring?

"Did you make that neat bandanna skirt you're wearing?" asked Alison.

"What about this cool blue-jeans purse?" asked Angela, holding it up.

"I like this pink fuzzy foot rug," said Amanda. "It's so cute!"

Julie sat up straight in her chair. The Water Fountain Girls actually *liked* her mom's junk!

"Julie and I just made that for her room," said Mom.

Amanda leaned forward and smiled at Julie. "You *made* that?" she mouthed, opening her eyes wide and giving her the thumbs-up sign.

"Do you sell Pet Rocks?" somebody asked.

"How about mood rings?" a boy in the front row said.

Suddenly, Julie's whole class had forgotten all about pilots and 747s and crash landings. They didn't even seem to care that it wasn't a dad up there talking. They were bubbling over with questions about what it was like to have your own store.

"I want to own a pet store when I grow up," said T. J. "And have giant lizards and rare albino frogs."

"You mean anybody can just start their own store?" asked Kimberly.

"Sure," said Mom. "I'm not saying it's easy. It's hard work—ask Julie. Some days I'm at my shop until ten o'clock at night. But it gives me a chance to do something creative, and I really like being my own boss."

Mom passed out mood rings and apple-seed bracelets to the entire class. The students immediately put them on, exclaiming, "Wow!" "Neat!" "You mean we get to keep these? For *free*?"

Julie's class didn't even seem to care that it wasn't a dad up there talking.

"It's called advertising," said Mom. "*Word-of-mouth* advertising. Maybe you'll come to shop at Gladrags now. Or tell a friend."

The whole class clapped when Mom was done. Julie glanced at her mood ring. It had changed from black to blue-green. The chart it came with said blue-green meant relaxed, calm. *Amazing,* thought Julie, realizing that was exactly how she felt.

During afternoon recess, all the kids could talk about was going to Gladrags. They crowded around Julie, asking her when the shop was open and where it was and if she could get stuff for free.

Word of mouth was . . . Julie's *mom* was the coolest parent at Career Day.

❀

"Hey, Julie!" T. J. called, slamming his locker shut from across the hall. "Coach Manley is posting the basketball sign-up sheet after school today."

In her excitement over Career Day, Julie had forgotten that today was the day for basketball team sign-ups. She hadn't even remembered to ask Mom about it. Julie could hardly sit still, waiting for the final bell to ring. As soon as school was out, she rushed down the hall toward the coach's office.

Coach Manley was a gym teacher. He had buzz-cut

hair like a GI Joe, a growly face, and a thick neck. Every time Julie passed the gym, he was shouting.

Julie looked for a sign-up sheet on the wall but didn't see one. She summoned her courage and knocked on the coach's door. She knew just how Dorothy felt knocking at the door of the Wizard of Oz.

"Enter," barked the coach.

Julie took a deep breath to steady herself. He reminded her of a dragon, about to breathe fire. "Hi, Mr. Manley," she said. "My name's Julie. Julie Albright. I'm a fourth-grader, and—"

"Yeah, yeah. You looking for the sign-up sheets? Got 'em right here."

"Really? That's great! So I'm the first one to sign up?"

"Yep. How many dozen should I put you down for?" asked Coach Manley.

"Dozen? Dozen what?"

"Cookies. For the basketball bake sale," said the coach, leaning back in his chair. "We're trying to raise money for new uniforms. How about I put you down for some choco-late chip cookies. My favorite."

"Cookies? I'm not here about cookies," Julie told him. "I'm here about the team. I want to be *on* the team. The basketball team."

"We don't have a girls' team at Jack London. We can

barely afford the boys' team. Why do you think we're having a bake sale?"

Julie took a deep breath. "Not the girls' team. The boys' team."

Coach Manley sat up. She had his full attention now. "Let me get this straight," he said slowly. "You want *me* to put *you* on the boys' basketball team."

Julie nodded, her heart pounding.

Coach Manley smiled and shook his head. "Young lady, the basketball team is for boys, and boys only. Got that?"

"I'm as good as the boys," Julie said softly. "Just give me a chance to try out. Please."

"Sorry. Answer's N-O, no. This is my team and I make the rules. In the spring, we'll have some intramural games—softball, tetherball, badminton. Maybe you can play one of those."

Julie shook her head. "That's not the same." She flushed and looked down at the floor, embarrassed to meet his eyes. A strange new feeling washed over her. It felt like a mixture of shame, frustration, and an emotion she couldn't quite identify. Was it anger?

She glanced up at the coach. He had turned back to his desk, signaling that it was time for her to leave. Her instinct was to run out of his office and never see him again. But something kept her feet firmly planted to the floor.

Finally, Coach Manley looked up. "I have work to do. This conversation is finished."

Julie felt her insides go all runny, like the yellow belly of a breakfast egg. As she turned to go, hot tears smarted at the back of her eyes. She ran all the way home, wind biting her ears and stinging her cheeks.

At Gladrags, Mom and Tracy had newspaper spread across the table and counter in the back, and they were gluing beads and buttons onto plain white lampshades.

"Hi, honey," said Mom. "I was telling your sister all about Career Day. You just missed some girls from your class. I've already had three new customers since my talk today."

Julie wondered if the new customers were the Water Fountain Girls. She looked at the table where her mom and sister were working. The green sports section of the newspaper was spread out, and a headline caught Julie's eye: "High School Girl Tackles Boys, School Board."

Julie pushed a pile of buttons off the article and began to read. When she finished, she turned to Mom. "See? This girl wasn't allowed to play on the school football team, so she went to court," said Julie, pointing to the news story. "The girl won her case and they had to let her play, because of this new law."

"Oh, yeah, we learned about that in civics class," said Tracy. "They passed some big federal law to make things more equal."

"I believe it's called Title Nine," said Mom. "But what does this have to do with you, Julie?"

"It's the basketball coach at school," Julie explained. "He won't let me play on the team because I'm a girl."

"He's a male chauvinist pig," said Tracy.

"Tracy!" Mom sounded a little shocked. "Where did you hear that?"

"Some people in tennis called Bobby Riggs a male chauvinist pig because he thought Billie Jean King couldn't beat him," Tracy replied. "Then she trounced him in a big match and proved that girls can be just as good as boys in sports."

Billie Jean King

"Look, honey," said Mom, smoothing out Julie's hair. "I don't see why you shouldn't be allowed to play on the team if that's what you really want. Let's talk this over with your dad when he gets back next week."

"I already talked to Dad about it, and even *he* doesn't want me to play on the boys' team," Julie told her. "But they don't have a girls' team. Besides, tryouts for all the positions are this week. Next week will be too late."

Julie grabbed the page with the article and rushed up

to her room. She scooped up her basketball and bounced it against the wall. *Thwump! Thwump!* She knew Mom didn't like her bouncing it in the apartment, but the satisfying thump of the ball helped ease the bundled-up feelings inside her.

Nobody ever asked her what *she* wanted. Divorce. *Thwump.* Moving. *Thwump.* Changing schools and leaving Ivy. *Thwump-thwump-thwump!* This morning, her horoscope had said "Create your own future by taking charge." Well, taking charge was what she was *trying* to do.

Julie stopped bouncing the ball and sat up straight. She wasn't going to give up. And they couldn't make her!

Let Girls Play, Too

❀ Chapter 4 ❀

The rest of the week at school seemed to drag on forever. On Friday, Julie was standing in front of her locker at the end of the day when she overheard the Water Fountain Girls whispering to each other.

"Shh! There she is. She's the one," said Alison.

"The one what?" asked Angela.

"Can you believe it?" said Alison. "She actually asked Coach Manley if she could be on the *boys'* basketball team!"

"She's a *tomboy*!" Amanda and Angela hissed, saying the word too loud on purpose.

Julie froze. She stuck her head deeper into her locker, pretending to look for her reading workbook. A voice came up behind her. "Just ignore them. You're good at basketball."

Julie pulled her head out of her locker and smiled gratefully at T. J. "Does Coach Manley already have the team picked out?" she asked.

"Nope. He's still choosing positions. I'm keeping my fingers crossed I'm a starter. Wish me luck."

"Luck," Julie said longingly, waving good-bye to T. J.

❁

Saturday morning Julie was reading her horoscope—
"Don't hesitate; today's the day to jump in"—when she
heard a knock on the door. Ivy was coming over for the
weekend, so Julie jumped up to answer the door.

"You're here!" Julie said, hugging Ivy. In the living
room, the two girls pushed boxes into the corner so
that Ivy could show Julie her latest floor routine.

"Did you know Olga Korbut was the first
gymnast to do a backward aerial somersault on
the balance beam?" Ivy asked as she turned
her handstand into a back limber.

Julie tried to copy the move, but as
soon as she got into a handstand, her
feet clomped to the floor.

Olga Korbut

"Girls!" called Mom. "What's going
on? Sounds like a stampede of elephants in there. Julie,
please tell me you're not bouncing that basketball inside."

"Don't worry, Mom," said Julie. "It's just handstands."

"Well, I don't want you two breaking your necks, either.
Why don't you run down to the deli and get us some lunch
meat for sandwiches, and we can have lunch in the shop.
I have lots of new beads, if you'd like to make bracelets."

"Oooh, beads!" said Ivy.

"Sure, Mom," said Julie.

As the girls walked down the hill toward Haight Street, Julie told Ivy all about Coach Manley and the basketball team. "After the coach wouldn't let me on the team, Tracy called him a pig," Julie confided.

"Whoa. I'd get in big trouble if I ever called a grown-up a pig," said Ivy.

"Not a *pig* pig. A *male chauvinist* pig. It's some big fancy word she learned from a tennis match. It means when boys think they're better than girls."

"I don't see why you'd want to play on a team with only creepy boys anyway," said Ivy. "They have smelly feet like pigs. Oink, oink!" Julie and Ivy pressed their noses into snouts and couldn't stop snorting and giggling.

At the corner, while they waited for the light to turn green, Julie saw Hank. He was carrying a clipboard, going up to cars stopped at the intersection, and talking to drivers through their car windows.

"Hey," said Ivy, "let's not cross here. Let's go down to the next light."

"But the market's right there," said Julie.

"I know, but I don't think we should walk past that

guy," said Ivy, pointing to Hank. "He's weird. He looks like a troll with all that orange hair."

"Oh, that's Hank. He's a friend of ours," said Julie. "I say hi to him all the time."

"I'm not supposed to talk to any strangers," said Ivy.

"Hank's not a stranger. Besides, Mom said I should be nice to him because he's one of those guys that was in the war. A Vietnam vet," Julie explained. "She says it's really hard when you've seen so many terrible, horrible things. Some people just can't get over it."

"Well, I don't know," said Ivy.

The light changed, and Julie took Ivy's hand as they crossed the street. Ivy switched to Julie's other side so that she wouldn't have to walk by Hank. But he had already spotted Julie.

"Hey, it's the new girl on the block," he called. "How do you like the new neighborhood?"

"Pretty well," Julie called back. "This is my friend Ivy, from my old neighborhood. We're going to the market to get stuff for lunch. Are you coming by the shop later?"

"No, not today. Too busy." Hank held out his clipboard. "I still need eighty-one more signatures."

"Signatures? For what?" Julie asked.

"For my petition," said Hank.

Even Ivy was curious. "A petition?" she asked.

"We're trying to get them to open the Veterans Center again. That's where all of us vets used to hang out. We liked to go there to chew the fat and play cards. The center was real important. For some of the homeless guys, it was the only meal they got all day."

"What happened to it?" asked Julie.

"Same ol' same ol'. Budget cuts. City said it didn't have enough money to keep it open." Hank shook his head. "But we're not giving up. If we each get a hundred and fifty signatures, we can take it to the bigwigs at the next board of supervisors meeting, and they have to open the issue back up for discussion."

"I sure hope you get enough signatures," said Ivy.

"Can anybody make a petition?" Julie asked him.

"Sure," said Hank. "It's a great way to get people to pay attention to your issue."

"And even if they said no about something, the petition might get them to change their minds?" asked Julie.

"Yep, that's what it's all about," said Hank. "Well, I gotta book," he said, tapping his clipboard. "Check you later."

"See you later, alligator," called Julie.

✿

As the girls ate their sandwiches, all Julie could think about was starting her own petition. After lunch, while Ivy began stringing glass beads to make a bracelet, Julie drew columns on a sheet of paper and numbered the lines up to one hundred fifty, just like Hank's petition.

"C'mon, Julie," said Ivy. "Don't you want to make bracelets? I'm going to make one for every day of the week!"

"Not right now," said Julie. "I'm making a petition." After all, her horoscope had said today was the day to jump in, so that's what she was doing. Julie wrote "Let Girls Play, Too" across the top of the page and drew basketballs and high-top sneakers in the margins. When she was done, she put on her roller skates.

"Hey, where are you going? I'm only up to Wednesday!" said Ivy.

"We can make bracelets any time," said Julie, waving her paper in the air. "C'mon, I need your help to get people to sign my petition."

Ivy put down her beads and trudged out the door after Julie, calling, "Wait up!"

Julie stopped at the corner. "Let's go ask that lady carrying the groceries across the street."

"For real? You're just going to walk right up to strangers and start talking to them? And tell them you want to be on a boys' basketball team?"

Julie felt her stomach do a nervous flip-flop. Maybe Ivy was right. Could she work up the courage to just walk right up to a total stranger? "Please, Ivy, just come with me."

"I don't think my parents would like me doing this," Ivy said.

Julie couldn't help wondering what her dad would say if he knew she was starting her own petition. She pushed the thought out of her mind. "Just help me get started," she pleaded. "I'll do all the talking, and if you don't like it, we can go home. I promise."

Ivy bit her lip. She did not look happy, but she followed her friend across the street.

"Excuse me," Julie called to a woman who was putting groceries into her trunk. Julie held out her clipboard for the woman to see. "Would you like to sign my petition? So I can be on the basketball team at my school?"

"Not interested," said the woman, looking annoyed.

"See? What did I tell you?" Ivy mumbled.

"Let's try that man coming out of the bakery," said Julie. "Hello! Would you like to sign my petition?"

"I'm in a hurry," said the man. "Good luck."

"Boy, he didn't even give me a chance to say what it's for!" said Julie, trying not to feel discouraged.

"How about that lady with the stroller? Maybe she likes kids," Ivy said.

Julie skated up to the lady and started off with, "Oh, what a cute baby!"

"Thanks," said the lady, beaming.

Julie held out her clipboard and explained her petition as the lady rocked the stroller back and forth.

"It's about time they started letting girls play the same sports boys get to play," said the lady. "Where do I sign?"

"Thanks a lot!" said Julie. "You're my first signature."

"I can see that. Well, best of luck to you."

"She was nice," Julie told Ivy.

"Good. Now can we go and finish making bracelets?"

"Ivy, that's only *one* signature. I need to get a hundred fifty."

Ivy stopped. "A hundred fifty! That could take a year!"

"C'mon, it's not that bad. At least let me get a few more. Hey, there's Hank—I bet he'll sign it."

Julie skated all over the neighborhood with Ivy trailing loyally behind. Every time the girls passed someone, Julie stopped and talked about her petition. Each time, it was like stepping out onstage at a school play, worrying she'd trip over a prop or forget her lines. But for every few people who wouldn't sign or didn't want to be bothered, Julie would find one who agreed with her.

Finally, Julie had almost one full column of signatures. She held up the clipboard triumphantly. "Look! Let's get just a few more."

"You've been saying that for hours," said Ivy. "Can't we go back now and make bracelets or do something *fun*?"

"I can't believe you think this is boring," said Julie.

"We've been doing this all afternoon," Ivy complained. "I hardly ever get to see you anymore, and I thought we were going to have *fun*."

Julie looked down at her petition. She had collected seventeen signatures, plus three blisters on her feet. She still had one hundred thirty-three more signatures to go. "Well, it's not dark yet, so I'm staying out a little longer."

"But you promised," said Ivy. "You said if I helped you get started, we could go home."

Julie threw her hands up in exasperation. "Don't you want my petition to work? You're my best friend. Don't you care if I get to play on the team?"

Ivy shrugged. "Not if it means we have to keep on doing this."

Julie spun around to face her friend. "How can you be so selfish?"

"Because you think playing basketball with a bunch of dumb old boys is more important than being friends with me!" Ivy turned and stomped off.

"Where are you going?" called Julie, skating after her.

"What do you care?" asked Ivy. Her back was stiff as

she stormed straight up the hill, faster than Julie could follow on skates.

"What about our sleepover?" Julie called after her. But Ivy turned the corner and disappeared from sight.

❁

The next day, Julie woke up exhausted. Her legs ached and her head felt as heavy as a bowling ball. Her first thought was that she should be having strawberry waffles with her used-to-be best friend Ivy. Instead, she sat up in bed and blinked back hot, angry tears.

Why was Ivy being so stubborn? Why couldn't she understand? What if somebody had told *her* she couldn't do gymnastics anymore?

Suddenly, Julie felt furious—at everything. If her parents hadn't divorced, she wouldn't have had to move. If she hadn't moved, she wouldn't be going to a new school with a basketball team that didn't allow girls. She'd have spent her Saturday with Ivy instead of asking people to sign a stupid petition . . .

The petition! Julie leaped up and snatched the clipboard from her desk. She yanked out the sheet with all the signatures, and *whhht!* She ripped the page in half and threw it on the floor.

Julie pulled on sweats and sneakers, grabbed her basketball, and ran outside. She dribbled—*bam bam bam*—hard and fast against the sidewalk.

"Hey, you're gonna wear a hole in the sidewalk, Sport!" called Hank, walking up Redbud Street.

Julie turned away and kept dribbling. Hank set down his coffee and bagel bag, came up behind Julie, and stole the ball right out from under her.

"Hey!" Julie chased after Hank, who dribbled down the sidewalk and juked right, then left, trying to fake her out. He spun into a driveway and lobbed up a hook shot as he passed under a rusty basketball rim attached above the garage.

"Nice shot!" said Julie, forgetting her bad mood. She scooped up the rebound and went for a layup herself.

They played hoops for several minutes, until Hank flopped down on the curb. "Haven't had my coffee, or I'd be able to keep up with you," he teased.

Julie perched on her ball, catching her breath.

"So, how's the petition going, Sport? You on that basketball team yet?"

"Huh," Julie snorted. "I don't even care about that anymore. It's too hard getting signatures and they'll never let me on the team anyway and besides, I lost my best friend over it," she said in one breath.

"Oh, so you don't mind not being on the team, then?"

Julie shrugged. "Doesn't matter. It's too late, anyway. I ripped up the petition."

Hank raised his eyebrows but said nothing. He gathered up his coffee and bagel and started to leave, then turned back to Julie. "Hey, you remember President Nixon?"

"Sort of. I remember when he resigned from being president," Julie said. She also remembered her parents arguing about him, but she didn't say that.

Hank nodded. "Well, I sure wasn't his biggest fan, but I remember he once said, 'A man isn't finished when he's defeated, he's finished when he quits.'" With that, Hank turned and headed up the street.

Julie went back up to her room and stared at the torn petition. She desperately wanted to be Ivy's friend again. But what would Ivy think if she knew Julie had torn up the very signatures she had dragged Ivy along for hours to get? Maybe Hank was right. What would she gain by giving up now?

Fitting the two halves back together, Julie smoothed out the petition, then opened her desk drawer and took out some tape.

❀

Now Julie carried the petition with her everywhere she went. She talked to people on her way to school. She asked the teachers, librarian, and school nurse if they'd sign. She showed it to T. J., who signed it. And she spent time after school walking around the neighborhood, asking neighbors if they would sign her petition.

But it wasn't the same without Ivy. When a woman with a parrot on her shoulder signed the petition and the parrot mimicked, "Sign here! Sign here!" Julie knew Ivy would have split her sides laughing. And when she reached one hundred signatures, she had no best friend to jump up and down with.

The next day after school, Julie went straight to Gladrags and banged her clipboard down on the workroom table.

"Why the long face?" asked Mom.

"I've been out there with my petition for over an hour and not one single person would sign it today."

"Any time you try to change something, it's going to be difficult," Mom said gently. "Not everybody thinks girls should play sports. A lot of people think games like football and basketball are just for boys."

"But that's not fair," said Julie.

"I know, honey. All I'm saying is, it can take a while for people to change their thinking. There was a time, only about fifty years ago, when people didn't even think women should be allowed to vote. It took a lot of hard work for that to change."

"I know," said Julie with a sigh. She stared glumly at the floor. "I miss Ivy, though. It's not as fun without her."

"I bet she misses you, too," said Mom. "You're just going to have to give it a little time."

Dumpsters and Hoopsters

✿ **Chapter 5** ✿

Thursday morning, Julie woke up early with a tingling of excitement. She dressed and ate quickly. If she hurried, she could get the last three signatures on her way to school.

When she got to school, Julie made a beeline for Coach Manley's office. The coach was on the phone. She clutched the petition in her hands, waiting for his conversation to end. It was almost time for the bell to ring. Standing in the open doorway, Julie held the paper up, trying to get his attention. She shuffled her feet. She coughed. She was about to knock when Coach Manley motioned her in. Then he saw the paper in her hand.

"Whatever it is, Albright, just leave it," he told Julie, covering the receiver with one hand.

"But I . . . it's really—"

"I said leave it. Can't you see I'm busy right now? Stop back later."

Looking down at the rumpled, taped-together page, Julie thought of all she'd been through to get those hundred and fifty signatures. She wanted to explain the significance of all those names. But she had no choice. She set the petition down on Coach Manley's desk and rushed to her classroom as the bell rang.

All day, Julie couldn't think of anything else. Finally, during social studies, she leaned over and whispered to T. J., "Do you think Coach Manley has read my petition?"

"Julie, T. J.?" said Ms. Hunter. "Is there something you'd like to share with the class about the Mississippi River?"

"Sorry, Ms. Hunter. I . . . I have a stomach ache," said Julie, which wasn't exactly a lie. "May I please have a hall pass to go see the nurse?"

Julie started down the hall to the nurse's office, but she couldn't stop her feet from heading straight to the gym office. She knocked at the open door. "Excuse me, Coach Manley?"

"What is it, Albright? Shouldn't you be in class?" the coach barked.

"Did you get a chance to read my petition?" Julie asked.

"I read it. Doesn't change a thing. Sports are for boys, not girls."

"But Coach, it's not just me anymore. A hundred and fifty people agree that I have a right to play on the team."

"I don't care if you show me a hundred and fifty *thousand* names," the coach told her. "They're all going in the same place." Right before her eyes, he balled up the petition and went for a basket . . . in the trash can.

Julie felt as if somebody had just punched her in the stomach.

"A piece of paper's never going to get you on this team," said the coach. "Now scram, before you get a demerit for being out of class."

As Julie headed back to her classroom, trembling with anger, a voice behind her boomed, "Young lady? Are you supposed to be in the halls right now?"

Julie stopped in her tracks. She turned and found herself looking right at Mr. Sanchez's pencil, which was pointing at *her* this time. His piercing eyes made her feel like a rabbit caught in an eagle's talons.

She held up her hall pass. "I'm on my way back to class," she squeaked.

"No wandering around now," he ordered. "Straight back to your classroom, you hear?"

"Yes, Mr. Sanchez," Julie said, turning to go. She hurried—but was careful not to run—back to class.

❁

"I'm so mad, I could scream," Julie told T. J. as soon as the final bell rang. "All my hard work, and he just scrunched up my petition as if it were an old hamburger wrapper."

"What are you gonna do now?" asked T. J.

"A piece of paper's never going to get you on this team," said the coach.

Julie paused. She'd been so certain her petition would work that she hadn't thought of a backup plan. There was only one thing to do. "Get my petition back."

"But how?"

"Come on. Let's go find Mr. Martin."

Mr. Martin, the janitor, was cleaning the cafeteria. He led Julie and T. J. out the back door and gestured to seven giant bags of trash.

"They're ready for the dumpster—but until then, they're all yours. Search away!" Mr. Martin said grandly, with a sweep of his arm.

Julie and T. J. dug right in. For twenty minutes, they were up to their elbows in milk cartons, pencil shavings, Popsicle-stick projects, and old worksheets.

"I don't see it anywhere," T. J. said finally. "And I better get to practice, or *I* won't be on the team either."

"Please, T. J. Only two more bags to go. Wait! What's this? This is it!" Julie held up the page in triumph. It was wrinkled and smeared with what looked like chocolate-milk drips, but Julie's heart leaped. It was like seeing an old friend. "Thanks a million, T. J." she said gratefully.

Julie knew what she had to do now. It would be harder than finding her petition in the trash, harder than facing

Coach Manley, harder than collecting all the signatures. Ignoring her pounding heart, Julie made herself walk down the hall to the front office. But when she got there, she froze outside the forbidding door—the door that said "Joseph Sanchez, Principal."

No turning back now, Julie told herself. The flutter inside her stomach was already whipping itself up into a tornado. She summoned all her courage and knocked on the door.

"Come in," a deep voice said.

Julie stepped into the principal's office, crossing the sea of gold carpet to stand in front of his desk, which was as shiny as a polished apple. Julie stood flagpole-straight, clutching her petition. She felt her hands grow moist. *You haven't done anything wrong,* she reminded herself.

The principal looked up from his desk. "What can I do for you, young lady?" he asked.

Julie took a deep breath and began to talk. She told him about wanting to play basketball, and how there was only a boys' team and the coach said no girls. She told him how good she was at basketball, how her father always said she could dribble like a Harlem Globetrotter, but now that her parents were, well, divorced, she couldn't play very often with her dad anymore. Then, suddenly running out of words, she handed Mr. Sanchez the wrinkled petition.

The principal looked at it. Julie could hear the clock

ticking as he read the long list of names. Finally, he peered over his reading glasses at Julie.

"So you're a hoopster. You know, I was a pretty good point guard myself, back in my high-school days. I used to dribble circles around some of the tallest guys on defense."

He wasn't angry with her! Julie felt herself breathe again.

"I can see this means a lot to you," Mr. Sanchez continued. "I can't make any promises, Julie. I'll have to talk this over with the school board. I'll get back to you next week."

At home that evening, Julie gushed with news of her eventful day.

"I'm proud of you, honey," said Mom, putting her arm around Julie and squeezing her tight.

"Weren't you scared talking to the principal?" asked Tracy, looking up from her homework.

"Yes," said Julie. "But he turned out to be nice. He used to play basketball, too."

"Hey, Mom, don't forget. Tell her about the thing." Tracy nodded toward the table by the front door.

The *thing*? Nervously, Julie followed her sister's glance, but she couldn't see anything unusual.

"Oops, I almost forgot in all the excitement," said Mom.

"A package came for you today."

"For me?" asked Julie.

"Special delivery!" Mom winked at Tracy as she handed Julie a small box.

The box was taped shut and rattled a little when Julie shook it. "It doesn't say who it's from," she said, puzzled.

"Just open it!" said Tracy.

Julie ripped open the box, only to find a paper-towel tube inside with the ends taped shut. She peeled the tape off one end and shook out a rolled-up sheet of paper that fell open like a scroll.

"What does it say, Jules?" asked Tracy.

"It's a petition," Julie said slowly. "Just like the one I made for basketball, with columns and numbers and everything."

At the top were big block letters. Julie read the words "Petition to Be Julie Albright's Best Friend. One–Ivy Ling. Two–Ivy Ling. Three–Ivy Ling. Four–Ivy Ling. Five–Ivy Ling . . ."

Julie unrolled the petition all the way to the floor. "She signed it one hundred and fifty times!"

"That's some friend you've got there," said Mom.

❀

Monday went by without a word from Mr. Sanchez. Then Tuesday. Every time Julie left her classroom, she kept an eye peeled. Instead of worrying that he'd point his accusing pencil in her direction, she was actually hoping to spot him, but Mr. Sanchez was nowhere to be seen. On Wednesday, Julie offered to take the attendance sheet to the office for Ms. Hunter, hoping that the principal would come out from behind that closed door. But he didn't.

Finally, on Thursday, just before the last bell was about to ring, an announcement came over the PA system. "Julie Albright, please report to the principal's office. Julie Albright."

"What'd you do?" Angela asked.

"She's in trouble!" said Alison.

It was all Julie could do not to sprint down the hall to the office. But at the same time, she felt a knot in the pit of her stomach, a small lump of dread. What if the school board had turned her down? What if the principal had talked to her dad? What if the answer was *no*?

Mr. Sanchez was standing in the doorway to his office. "Hello, Julie," he said, motioning for her to come in and sit down. He cleared his throat. "After careful consideration, I've determined that we're not in a position to start a girls' basketball team at this time." He paused. Julie's heart sank.

"However, I've also determined that to be in full

compliance with Title Nine, our school must allow you
to play on the boys' basketball team." He smiled. "So,
that makes you the newest member of the Jack London
Jaguars."

Julie jumped up out of her seat. She could hardly keep
from throwing her arms around him. Wait till she told T. J.!

"Now, before you get too excited, I'm not finished yet.
Let me stress that some people will disagree with this
decision, and I don't want any trouble, on or off the court.
I've spoken with Coach Manley, and you will report di-
rectly to him if you have any problems."

Julie nodded. "Thank you, Principal Sanchez," she said
politely. But in her mind, she was already dribbling through
the open doors of the gym and out onto the court.

Walking home that afternoon, Julie took a shortcut and
realized for the first time that she knew the route by heart.
She no longer had to concentrate on street names, land-
marks, or left and right turns. Her feet practically bounced
with the good news. She couldn't wait to tell Mom and

Tracy, knowing how excited they'd be for her. Ivy, too.

She wasn't sure about Dad. Julie hoped he'd be happy for her. It was true that he hadn't liked the idea of her playing on a boys' team—but wasn't he the one who'd taught her how to shoot hoops in the first place?

Julie imagined bursting through the front door of their old house and announcing the good news to her whole family, all together, and then racing across the street to tell Ivy. Unfortunately, that wasn't the way it would be. But she wasn't going to let it spoil her good mood.

As Julie turned the corner onto Redbud Street, she saw the welcoming lights beneath the front awning of Gladrags, glowing as if in celebration. Mom would be there, bracelets jangling as she arranged items on a shelf or waited on a customer. And Tracy would be home any minute, tossing her tennis racket on the kitchen table, kicking off her sneakers, fixing herself a snack. In the living room, the prism hanging in the front window would be catching the last light of day, splashing rainbows everywhere, all around the room.

Julie broke into a run, heading home.

Homework!

✿ Chapter 6 ✿

School was now in full swing at Jack London
Elementary, and Julie discovered that she had
more to worry about than basketball.

Homework. She had never had so much homework before
in her life! At her old school, all she'd had to do for homework was fun stuff, like reading *Charlotte's Web* or doing
a word search. But Ms. Hunter's fourth-grade class had
book reports to write, vocabulary words to memorize, and
geography maps to draw. And now, Ms. Hunter had just announced a new assignment—a "family project" that would
stretch out over several weeks. Julie winced. Families were
not Julie's favorite topic right now—not since the divorce.

Julie studied Ms. Hunter's precise handwriting on the
blackboard, trying to imitate her teacher's loopy cursive
writing as she copied the topic into her own notebook.

The Story of My Life

Just then, T. J. slid a note over to her. Opening the note
in her lap, Julie sneaked a peek at it.

The Story of My Life is too much homework!

Julie grinned at T. J. Then she turned her attention back to her notebook and carefully copied the complete homework assignment from the blackboard:

My First Memory

When My Mom Was My Age

When My Dad Was My Age

The Best Thing That Ever Happened to Me

The Worst Thing That Ever Happened to Me

Julie's first memory, when she was three or four, was sneaking into her parents' room and jumping on the big bed when nobody was looking. The Best Thing That Ever Happened was easy—getting to play on the boys' basketball team. It was the Worst Thing that Julie could not imagine writing about. Julie didn't even like *thinking* about her parents' divorce.

"Class," Ms. Hunter was saying, "this project is not about sitting at your desk and telling me what you remember. I would like all of you to be reporters here. Interview your family members and find out about them. Ask them questions. Learn something new about the people closest to you.

"I want at least one page on each of the topics," Ms. Hunter went on. "You'll also give an oral report to the class about all you've learned."

An oral report to the class! This assignment just kept getting worse. It was bad enough that Julie's parents were divorced, but did she have to tell the whole class about it?

Julie decided she would have to come down with a bad case of The Dog Ate My Homework. Or in her case, The Rabbit Ate My Homework. Maybe she'd come down with writer's cramp. Or writer's block, whatever that was. Julie pictured a gigantic toy block sitting on top of her hand, weighing it down so that she couldn't write.

When Julie went to her locker at the end of the day to grab her gym bag and head for basketball practice, she heard some of her classmates buzzing about their projects. Sure enough, it was the Water Fountain Girls, who loved to chatter and gossip.

"I can't wait to work on my family project," said Alison. "The best thing ever in my family was when we all went together on a vacation last summer to the Grand Canyon."

"I'm going to tell how my mom and dad went scuba diving for their tenth anniversary and brought back a real shark's tooth for me and my brothers," said Angela.

"My mom's an identical twin, so when my mom and dad were getting married, they played a trick on him and my dad almost married my aunt!" said Amanda. "We still tease him about how my aunt was almost my mom. I could tell that story."

Julie sighed. It was so easy for them. They all had regular families and happy, funny stories.

Maybe she could make up a pretend story about the Worst Thing That Ever Happened to her. Then she wouldn't have to write about the divorce for the whole entire class.

"Earth to Julie," T. J. said, waving his hand in front of her frowning face. "Ready for practice?"

"I was just thinking," said Julie. "About our family report."

"Don't remind me," said T. J. "What are you going to write for the Best Thing Ever?"

"Easy," said Julie. "Getting to play on the basketball team. Being one of the Jaguars is definitely the Best Thing That Ever Happened to Me."

"Speaking of basketball, you know how Coach Manley gets if we're late for practice," said T. J. "We'd better hurry, or we'll both be writing about getting kicked *off* the team for the Worst Thing That Ever Happened."

That afternoon, Dad picked Julie up after school and drove her to his house for the weekend. Funny how she thought of the house she grew up in as *Dad's* house now, Julie reflected.

When they arrived at Dad's, Julie headed for the back door. "I'm going to bring Nutmeg inside." Now that Julie no longer lived there, the rabbit lived in a hutch in the backyard, except when Julie visited.

"I already brought her in," said Dad. "She's upstairs in your room."

"Thanks, Dad," said Julie, racing up the stairs two at a time. She burst into her old bedroom and was surprised, as always, by how different it looked from before. No rolltop desk, no bookcase, no beanbag chair. This room, these four walls, this shaggy carpet were all she'd known for nine years—her whole life. But nothing felt familiar anymore. When she called softly to Nutmeg, her voice seemed to echo, bouncing back to her off the blank walls. Julie scooped up Nutmeg from her basket in the corner where the desk used to be and ran back downstairs, keeping ahead of the empty feeling that the room gave her now.

While Dad peeled an apple, Julie perched on the edge of the kitchen counter and dangled an apple peeling in front of Nutmeg's sniffing nose. Nutmeg's whiskers twitched and quivered with excitement.

"You're awfully quiet this

afternoon," Dad said. "Everything okay at school? How's basketball going?"

Julie hesitated. Dad had taken the news well when she told him that she got on the boys' team, but he hadn't yet been able to attend any of her games. And Julie didn't want to tell him that the boys on the other teams sometimes called her mean names just because she was a girl. Instead, she told him about the three steals she'd made in the last game.

"Oh, man. I wish I'd been there," said Dad.

"We have a big game in two weeks, against the Wildcats, and I'm kind of nervous about it," Julie told him. "Will you be able to come watch me play?"

"You bet I'll be there," said Dad.

"I also have a gigantic school project I have to start working on," Julie sighed.

"You don't sound very happy about it," said Dad.

"It's just that, well . . ." She didn't quite know how to explain to Dad why it was hard for her to write about her family. She didn't want to make him feel bad. "It's just that my teacher gives so much homework," Julie said finally. She described the project and how she was supposed to interview everyone in her family. Picking up a ketchup bottle, she spoke into it. "Reporting to you live from the home of Daniel Albright, world-famous pilot. He has just returned from a daring adventure—"

"Hey, wait a second," said Dad. "Hold it right there, Ace. I have an idea." He disappeared into the den and came out holding both hands behind his back.

"What is it?" asked Julie.

"Something I got for you in Japan. I was planning to put it away for Christmas, but it seems to me you could really use it for your school project. On the other hand, maybe we should wait," Dad teased.

"Dad! I think it's a great idea to give it to me *now*!" Julie leaped up and faked right, then left, using her fancy footwork from basketball to try to grab whatever Dad was holding behind his back.

"Time out! Foul!" Dad called, blocking Julie. "Okay, okay, I give up." Dad brought his hands out from behind his back, presenting the item he'd been hiding.

Julie looked at it. "What is it, a transistor radio?" she asked.

"It's a portable tape recorder," said Dad. "With a microphone and everything. It'll be great for your interviews, don't you think?" Dad pointed to the buttons. "See, if you plug in the microphone here, and put in a blank tape, you can use it to record people."

"You mean I can talk and sing into it and stuff?" asked Julie. "Then play it back and hear myself on tape?"

"Yup," said Dad.

"This is so boss! Thank you, Dad," Julie said, hugging him. "Can I go over to Ivy's and show her my new tape recorder?"

"Be back by dinner!" Dad called.

But Julie was already halfway out the door.

"Hey, Ivy!" Julie said, bursting through the door as soon as her friend opened it. "Look what my dad just gave me. A tape recorder!" Julie held it up.

"Far out," said Ivy, imitating Tracy and teenagers they heard on TV. "Let's go to my room and try it." Ivy was sucking a grape Popsicle, and she expertly caught a juicy purple drip.

"Oooh, keep slurping your Popsicle real loud and I'll tape it." Julie turned on the tape recorder and said, "Testing, testing, one, two, three, testing," into the microphone. Then she held it up to Ivy.

Slurp, slurp. Ivy exaggerated the slurpy-lurpy sounds.

"Now let's rewind and see if it worked." Julie played back the tape, and the two girls collapsed onto Ivy's bed, laughing.

"What else can we tape?" Julie asked.

"I know—let's make some sound effects," said Ivy. "Like they do in movies."

"Great idea," said Julie. Putting pairs of wooden-soled clogs onto their hands, the girls clip-clopped against the floor to sound like a giant tromping down the stairs. A squeaky door sounded like a mouse when Julie held the microphone up to its hinges. For rain, they turned on the shower.

"The toilet!" said Julie. "Pretend you're about to get flushed down the toilet."

"Help!" cried Ivy. "Save me! A giant whirlpool is about to—" *Ker-plushhh!* Ivy flushed the toilet while Julie held out the microphone. They bit their lips to keep from laughing.

"Let's hear it," said Julie, hitting the *rewind* button. They listened to their entire collection of sound effects. When it came to the flushing toilet, Ivy said, "That sounds like Yosemite Falls!" They played it over and over, laughing harder each time.

"Hey, Ivy, I gotta go," Julie said finally. "Dad said to be home by dinnertime."

"See you later," said Ivy. "And don't forget to blink your lights tonight when you go to bed, and I'll blink mine."

"I won't forget," Julie told her friend.

❀

Julie and Ivy played with the tape recorder all day
Saturday. But after breakfast on Sunday, Julie realized that
her weekend with Dad was almost over and she still hadn't
interviewed him for her school project.

She popped a new blank tape into the recorder. "Go
ahead, Dad. Tell me a story about when you were my age."

"Let's see if I can remember that far back, to the Stone
Age."

"C'mon, Dad, this is serious," Julie said.

"Okay," said Dad, settling into his favorite chair.
"When I was in the fourth grade, growing up in Duluth,
Minnesota, money was tight and none of us could afford a
bike. So my buddies and I fished a real junker out of the
trash and fixed it all up. We painted it black and yellow and
called it the Hornet. We spent a whole summer swapping
that bike around. Our favorite thing was building ramps so
we could do jumps. One day, just as I took the jump, my
pants got snagged in the chain and I lost my balance. I went
head over handlebars, landing all twisted up like a pretzel."

"Whoa! Were you hurt bad?" Julie asked.

"Well, I broke my foot, and I had to wear a clunky
cast the rest of the summer. Couldn't take a bath for over
a month, which I didn't much mind when I was ten, but
I couldn't go swimming, either."

"Did you have to use crutches? Did it heal up okay?"

"Yup, I did get pretty fast on crutches. And the doc told me something interesting that I've never forgotten," said Dad, taking off his shoe. "In the spot where the bone was broken, it actually knits itself back together stronger than before." He took Julie's hand and ran her finger over a small bump on the top of his foot.

"That's all that's left from the break?" Julie asked.

"That's all," said Dad.

Meet Charlotte

❖ **Chapter 7** ❖

The next day after school, the string of brass bells jingled as Julie came in through the front door of Gladrags, calling, "Hello? Anybody home?" She made her way past racks of ponchos and peasant shirts and shelves of sandalwood incense.

"Hi, honey," Mom called from the back room. "Good timing. I was just fixing myself a cup of tea. How was school today?"

"Fine, Mom. Is now a good time to interview you for my school project?"

"Sure, but if any customers come—"

Julie was already dashing upstairs. She grabbed her tape recorder and hurried back down to the shop.

Julie held out the microphone, and Mom began telling her all about the time when she was ten, growing up on an apple farm in Santa Rosa, north of San Francisco.

"I got a horse named Firefly

for my tenth birthday, and of course I couldn't wait to ride her. I'd begged and pleaded for a whole year, wanting a horse of my own. But before I even climbed into the saddle, the horse got spooked and acted all crazy, rearing and jumping and bucking."

"Whoa," Julie whispered.

"She broke away from your grandpa, who was holding the reins, and ran out through the garden and around the apple orchard. Finally she stepped on her reins, and that stopped her."

Just as Mom was finishing her story, Tracy came in and plunked a towering armload of schoolbooks on the table. "Shh!" Julie pointed to the tape recorder, holding a finger to her lips and frowning.

"Is it safe to talk now?" Tracy asked impatiently when Mom finished. Julie pressed the *stop* button and nodded. Tracy held up a leafy plant spilling out of a milk carton.

"What's that?" asked Julie.

"Meet Charlotte, my new roommate," Tracy said.

Mom laughed. "Your new roommate is a spider plant?"

"Oh, I get it," said Julie. "Charlotte, like the spider in *Charlotte's Web*?"

"Exactly," said Tracy.

"Who gave you a plant for a present? A boy?" Julie teased.

"No! It's not a present. It's a project we're doing in biology. All the kids in the class got their own spider plants. I have to take care of it and keep a daily journal where I track how much water it gets and stuff like that."

"Wow, they gave you a real live plant at school?" Julie exclaimed. "All I ever got was a potato. We made potato people in art class once."

"Well, this plant is worth twenty points of my grade, so it better not croak."

Julie picked up the microphone and clicked *record*. She pointed it at Tracy. "It helps plants grow if you play music or sing to them. Why don't you sing 'Eensy Weensy Spider' to Charlotte?"

"On tape? You have got to be kidding. I'm not singing to a plant."

"C'mon, I could use it in my family report. I have a school project, too, you know."

"Turn that thing off," Tracy said, reaching over and pressing the *stop* button. "Mom, do you have any pots or planters around? I have to transplant Charlotte."

"Let's see," said Mom, looking around the workroom. "Check that box on the bottom shelf."

Tracy rummaged through the box. "Hey, what's this?" she asked, holding up a clay hippo.

"Aw, that's cute," said Julie. "What is it—a candy dish with legs?"

"No, it's actually for a plant," said Mom. "A guy here in San Francisco makes them, and he gave me one as a sample, to see if I'd sell them at the shop."

"It's perfect! I bet I'll even get extra credit for having such a cute planter," Tracy crowed. "Thanks, Mom."

Julie grabbed her tape recorder and followed Tracy up the back stairs into the kitchen.

"Stop following me with that thing," said Tracy.

"I'm not following you. I just need to tape you for my school report on my family."

"Can't you see I have more important things to worry about right now? Help me spread newspapers on the kitchen table so I can repot my plant."

Julie spread out the newspapers while Tracy carefully lifted the plant from the milk carton and transferred it into the hippo pot. She poured the spilled dirt around the plant and gently patted the soil. In no time, Charlotte had a happy new home on Tracy's desk.

Julie was singing a song into her microphone and dancing around her room after dinner when Tracy poked her head in the doorway. "I hate to interrupt the concert," she said, "but Mom says she could really use our help down in the shop. She got a whole shipment of night-lights today."

Dropping the microphone on the bed, Julie followed Tracy down the back steps into the shop, where Mom had set two big boxes on the worktable.

"Girls, can you unpack these night-lights? Be careful with the seashells," said Mom. "We have to put them together first, and then price each one."

Julie lifted some shells out of the box. "Wow, look at this shell," she said, holding up a round purplish globe.

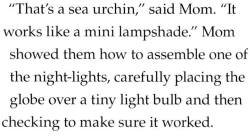 "That's a sea urchin," said Mom. "It works like a mini lampshade." Mom showed them how to assemble one of the night-lights, carefully placing the globe over a tiny light bulb and then checking to make sure it worked.

The girls set to work assembling the night-lights and putting on price stickers. Julie loved handling the pretty shells and trying to decide which shape she liked best. What fun it was to be helping Mom in the shop after hours! It occurred to Julie that if her parents hadn't split up, her mother might never have opened Gladrags. Julie sighed, confused. How could she feel so torn between the way things used to be and the way her life was now?

This Little Piggy

❁ Chapter 8 ❁

he next day after basketball practice, Coach Manley called the team into a huddle. "Johnson, work on that defense inside the key. Albright, I've seen notes in class passed faster than your bounce pass. McDermott, what's with all the fouls? Tomorrow you'd better be over your case of the clumsies. That's it, players. See you tomorrow."

As soon as Coach Manley was out of earshot, T. J. muttered, "What got into Coach today? I feel like I just ran a marathon or something."

"What's wrong with my defense, anyway?" complained Paul Johnson, point guard for the Jaguars.

"And I had one of my best passes ever," Julie chimed in. "I think Coach Manley needs glasses."

"He's just uptight about playing the Wildcats. The big game is in two weeks, and he thinks we're not ready to take them on," said Tommy McDermott, the team captain.

"At this rate, we're going to be too *tired* to play the Wildcats," said T. J., and everybody laughed.

"I hear they have this one fifth-grader who's practically

six feet tall," said Tony Monteverdi, who played center. "They call him Dunk because he can jam balls right through the hoop."

"Yeah, he thinks he's the next Kareem Abdul-Jabbar," said Brian Hannigan, the team's forward. Brian was five foot eight himself, but even he looked worried.

"Great," said Julie. "I bet he's just going to love playing against a team with a girl."

"Hey, don't go thinking that way," said Paul. "You're one of the best ball handlers we've got on this team. We don't call you Cool Hand Albright for nothing."

"Really? You guys gave me a nickname?"

"Are you kidding?" said T. J. "You can dribble rings around half this team."

All the way home, Julie couldn't stop thinking about the Wildcats. Just the thought of going up against the legendary Dunk made her shiver. To chase away the goose bumps, Julie recalled Paul's words. *One of the best ball handlers.* She could still feel the warm glow of the compliment.

Cool Hand Albright. Her very own nickname!

On Saturday morning, Julie set up an obstacle course on the sidewalk with a laundry basket, an empty bucket, and a family-size box of laundry detergent. She weaved her way in and out of the obstacles, switching hands, practicing her dribbling, then pretending to palm off the ball in a bounce pass to an imaginary player.

"Hey! Whatya doing?" a voice asked. Tracy.

"Practicing my bounce pass. Coach Manley told me it needs work."

"Well, it looks pretty good to me," said Tracy cheerfully. "Want me to stand in? You can go through the course and then pass the ball off to me."

"Hey, wait a minute," said Julie suspiciously. Tracy, offering to help her? "I'm not doing the dishes for you tonight, if that's what you're thinking."

"No, of course not," said Tracy. "C'mon, why don't you start dribbling, and then pass the ball to me."

"Well, okay, thanks. Ready?" asked Julie.

For the next several minutes, Julie weaved, turned, faked, and drove the ball this way and that, bounce-passing it to Tracy, who passed it right back. In the scramble, Julie knocked into the box of detergent, spilling white powder all over the sidewalk. Between bounce passes, Tracy tried to steal the ball, but Julie was too fast.

"Time out!" Tracy called, winded. Panting, the two girls sat down on a nearby front step.

"How would you like to do some babysitting?" Tracy asked casually.

"I'd love to, but Mom says I'm too young," Julie replied. "Why? You know somebody who needs a babysitter?"

"Umm—sort of."

"Who?" Julie bolted upright, excited by the possibility of her first job. "Do you think Mom'll let me? How much do they pay?"

"Well, since it's your first time, it would have to be for free. You know, to get experience. Then you work up to the big bucks."

"I don't know," said Julie, leaning back on her elbows. "On *The Brady Bunch,* Marcia and Greg get paid just to babysit their own brothers and sisters."

"Well, this isn't *The Brady Bunch,*" said Tracy. "Could you start later today?"

"You mean it? For real? How old is the kid? What's the kid's name?"

Tracy glanced sideways at Julie. "Um, Charlotte?" she said, making it sound like a question.

"It's your plant!" Julie said in disbelief. "You want me to babysit a dumb old plant? That's why you're being all nice and helping me with basketball and everything?"

"C'mon, Jules, you'd really be helping me out. It's super easy—you'd hardly have to do anything. Just go in my room and check on it a couple of times over the weekend. If the soil feels dry, give it a little water. And if you notice anything different or unusual, just write it down so that I can record it in my science journal."

"I can't. Ivy's coming for a sleepover, and I might forget. Besides, why can't you do it yourself?"

Tracy lowered her voice to a conspiratorial whisper. "I'm going to my friend Jill's house for the weekend, and her brother has a VW bug. Have you ever heard of Volkswagen stuffing? We're going to see how many kids we can pile into his car. It'll be like playing Twister times ten."

"That sounds weird," said Julie.

"It's going to be groovy," said Tracy. "And Jill invited me to spend the night at her house. I really want to go, but I'll get points taken off if I skip two whole days in my journal."

"Okay, I'll do it. But it'll cost you. Two dollars."

"Two dollars! Are you nuts? For maybe watering it once and making sure it doesn't croak?"

"Take it or leave it," said Julie, crossing her arms to show that her mind was made up.

"One dollar," said Tracy.

"Deal," said Julie.

"The eensy-weensy spider went up the water spout," Julie sang to the plant on her bedroom windowsill. Ivy joined

in, adding all the hand motions that went with the song.

"Tell me again why we're singing to a plant?" Ivy asked.

"It's for Tracy's science project. She asked me to watch her plant this weekend, but I was afraid I'd forget, so I just brought it in here. There's more sunlight in my room, anyway," said Julie. "And I read in a magazine that if you sing to plants or play music around them, they grow faster."

"Really? That sounds wacky," said Ivy.

"I know," Julie admitted. "But wouldn't it be great if Tracy came back and her plant had grown a whole inch? She'd get extra credit for sure. Let's sing it again!"

"Okay, one last time," Ivy agreed. "Then let's go do something outside."

"I know—this time I'll tape us singing!" said Julie. "Then I can just play the tape for Charlotte."

When the girls were finished singing, Julie pressed the *play* button and then picked up her basketball. "You want to go shoot some hoops?" she asked Ivy.

"Sure," said Ivy. "Let me get my shoes on."

"Think fast!" Julie said, tossing a pass to Ivy. But Ivy had bent down to pull on her boots. The ball hit the dresser, and then zinged off the corner, heading right for the open window.

"Noooooo!" Julie dove across the bed, lunging to save the ball from going out the window. The basketball thumped against the windowsill, then bounced into Julie's hands. "Whew—got it!"

Ivy stared at the window in horror.

Crash.

"What was that?" Julie followed Ivy's gaze to the open window—and empty windowsill.

For a split second, Julie's mouth gaped open in shock. Then Julie and Ivy rushed over to the window and peered down at the sidewalk below. Charlotte lay in a jumbled heap on the ground. Dirt was scattered all over the sidewalk. The clay hippo was smashed to pieces.

In a blur, Julie and Ivy raced down the back steps and out onto the sidewalk.

"Oh, no!" said Julie in disbelief. "What are we going to do?" She picked up the spider plant, turning it in her hand. Many of the long, blade-like leaves were crushed and broken, and the roots looked pale and limp.

"Maybe the roots are still okay," Ivy said hopefully. "And we can clean up all this dirt. It's probably still perfectly good dirt."

"But the pot—we've got to put it back together."

Ivy shook her head. "There are too many pieces. We'll never be able to glue it."

"Then we'll have to find another pot just like it," said Julie, picking up the pieces.

"Does your mom have more pots like this at her shop?" Ivy asked.

"No, that's the problem. This one was just a sample," Julie explained.

"I've seen them at the Five-and-Ten Shop in Chinatown," said Ivy. "My mom has one that's a frog."

"Hey, there's a Five-and-Ten Shop right down on Haight Street," said Julie, brushing the last of the dirt off the sidewalk. "I'll tell my mom we're going. Come on!"

On Haight Street, the girls rushed past the bead shop and the record store. "Mom's told me a million times not to play basketball in the apartment. Now I know why," Julie murmured. She peeked at Charlotte, who lay in a soft bag that Mom had made from an old pair of jeans. The plant looked a bit crushed. "We better hurry."

At the Five-and-Ten Shop, Julie went down an aisle filled with Halloween candy and spooky decorations. "There's the plant section," she said, motioning to Ivy. They walked past rows of begonias and African violets, looking for the pots.

"Over there!" said Ivy. They scanned the cluttered shelf, searching for a planter in the shape of a hippo like Tracy's.

"They have bunnies and puppies, cows and kittens," said Julie. "There just has to be a hippo." She began lifting out all the pots stacked behind the front row and setting them on the floor.

"May I help you?" asked a tall woman wearing a blue smock with a name tag that said "Glenda."

"Sorry," said Julie. "We'll put these all back. We're just looking for a hippo."

"It's an emergency," Ivy explained.

"The puppies are very cute," said Glenda. "They're our most popular item."

Both girls shook their heads. "It has to be a hippo."

"I don't think we've ever carried a hippo, but we might be able to order one," Glenda offered.

"That won't work," Julie explained. "This is my sister's plant, for a school project. She had it in a hippo planter, and I broke it!"

"Oh, I think I'm getting the picture. Tell you what. We have a few piggies left, over here," Glenda said, lifting one down from a high-up shelf. "Don't you think it looks sort of like a hippo?"

Julie looked at Ivy. Ivy shrugged. "It's pretty close," she told her friend.

"We could even call it Wilbur, like the pig in *Charlotte's Web*. But not to Tracy, of course," said Julie. She turned to Glenda. "Okay, we'll take it."

"Would you like me to pot the plant for you?" Glenda

asked, glancing at the limp plant in Julie's hand. "I can trim off some of those broken leaves."

"Really? That'd be great. Does it cost extra?" Julie asked.

"Not for emergencies." Glenda winked at Julie. "I'll have to take it in the back. Why don't you girls look around and come back in fifteen minutes?"

While they waited, Julie and Ivy wandered over to the pet section. They tried to get the parakeets to talk, and they gazed at the hermit crabs, hoping to catch one changing shells. At the turtle tank, they made up names for some of the baby turtles, like Slow Poke and Cutie Pie.

"It's probably been fifteen minutes," said Julie after a bit. "Let's go and see if Wilbur and Charlotte are ready."

At the counter, Glenda handed them the repotted spider plant. "Well, I can't say it's as good as new, but it should pull through. Be sure to give it a good drink when you get home."

"Thanks a million!" said Julie as she paid for the pot. "It looks better already."

"And the leaves cover up the pot, so you can't really tell it's not a hippo," said Ivy.

"Be careful, now," said Glenda. "You don't want to make any more trips to the plant hospital today."

The girls smiled and waved as they headed out the door. "Time for this little piggy to go home!" said Julie.

❁

The next afternoon, Julie and Ivy sat at the kitchen table, riveted to the tick-tick-ticking of the cat's tail on the Kit-Kat Klock hanging above the stove.

"Quit looking at the clock. You're making me nervous," said Julie, turning back to their game of Chinese checkers.

"The way the cat's eyeballs move back and forth, I feel like he's staring at me," said Ivy. "Do you think Tracy's going to know something happened to her plant?"

"I hope not. Because if that plant dies, she might flunk her assignment."

"Uh-oh," said Ivy as she jumped a marble.

"Speaking of assignments, one *good* thing about all this is I have a new idea for my report. Worst Thing Ever: knocking Charlotte out the window." Julie moved a marble. "Remember, when Tracy gets here, just act natural."

Five minutes later, the front door opened, and Tracy called out, "Hey, everybody. I'm ba-ack!"

"Whew, it sounds like she's in a good mood," Julie whispered to Ivy.

"Anybody home?" Tracy called.

"We're in the kitchen," Julie called back. She swallowed

hard as her sister entered the room.

"Hi, Ivy," said Tracy.

"So, did you and your friends break any world records?" asked Julie. "You know, for the number of people in a VW?"

"I think we broke the record for the number of *squished* people," said Tracy. "So, anything happening around here?"

"No!" Julie glanced nervously at Ivy, who was rolling a marble between her fingers. "What makes you say that?"

"Nothing, I was just asking," said Tracy. She picked up her backpack. "Well, I'm going to go change."

"She didn't even ask about Charlotte," Julie whispered when Tracy had left the room.

Suddenly they heard a shriek. Tracy's door flew open and she yelled down the hall, "Julie, what on earth did you do?"

Julie hurried to Tracy's room, with Ivy right behind her. "What do you mean?" she asked. "What's wrong?"

Tracy pointed at Charlotte on her desk. "My plant looks *smaller*. Like it shrunk. And the tips of the leaves are turning brown! Are you sure you watered it?" Tracy asked.

"Positive. We held it under the faucet for like five minutes. Didn't we, Ivy?"

Ivy nodded. "Yeah, and we put it in Julie's window so it would get more sunlight. We sang to it, too."

"Great, you probably overwatered it. Plants can drown, you know. And it's not supposed to be in direct sunlight.

No wonder the tips are brown!"

"Maybe some music will help," said Julie. "We made Charlotte a tape—want us to play it?"

"Never mind," said Tracy with a heavy sigh. "I'll just have to put these observations in my journal."

Julie and Ivy wandered back to the kitchen table and gazed at the Chinese checkers board. "I think it's your move," said Julie, but the game no longer seemed fun.

"Hey, she didn't even notice Wilbur," said Ivy.

"Yeah," said Julie. "That's good, at least."

The Big Game

Chapter 9

Three more days. Two more days. One more day. Julie deliberately marked a red crayon X through each day leading up to the big game with the Wildcats, the Thursday that had been circled on her calendar for the last three weeks.

Yikes—the big game was today!

"All ready?" asked Mom, poking her head into Julie's room. "I made French toast this morning."

"Thanks, Mom." Julie's voice came out in a tiny squeak.

"Nervous?" asked Mom.

"A little," said Julie. "Excited, too. I just wish you could be there."

"I know, honey. I'm disappointed, too. Of all the days for the bank to schedule a big meeting to talk about my business loan. But Dad'll be there. I'm sure he'll take some pictures. And you can tell me all about it, play by play."

Mom drove Julie to school that morning and gave her an extra-special squeeze before Julie got out of the car. "Remember, take a deep breath, and just do your best. That's all anybody can ask."

"See ya later, Hoopster," said Tracy, sliding out of the front bench seat so Julie could climb out. "Go easy on those boys, now. Don't make those Wildcats look too bad." Julie giggled. "I'll try to be there by the second half, if tennis practice is over," Tracy told her.

"Bye!" Julie waved.

"One, two, three . . . Go, Jaguars!" Julie, T. J., and the other players broke from the huddle, and the big game was on. The opening jump ball went to the Wildcats, and it was all the Jaguars could do to keep up. The crowd was already up out of their seats, cheering as the ball moved up and down the court.

"Defense, defense!" Coach Manley yelled to his players.

Julie double-teamed with T. J. to try to block the tall kid, Wildcat Number 16, also known as Dunk.

"Hey, twenty-two, forget your cheerleading pom-poms?" Dunk snickered as he stole the ball from Julie. Then he elbowed right past her, shoving her out of the way. It was the third time he had fouled her, but the ref had only called a foul once.

"Hey, no fair," Julie called.

"That's a foul, 'fraidy-cats!" T. J. shouted.

Julie knew her dad worried about rough play, and he would not be happy about it. She tried to spot him in the stands, but the game was moving fast and she couldn't find him.

Julie ran downcourt. With a minute left in the first half, the Jaguars were down by six points, but they had the ball.

"Hey, ballerina," called Number 16. "Where's your tutu?"

Julie gritted her teeth. She had to concentrate, focus, do everything Coach Manley had taught them in practice to block out distractions and drive the ball so that her team could score.

Dunk was on her again, so she quickly passed the ball to T. J. He was instantly surrounded and had to pass it back. Just as the ball reached Julie's hands, Dunk lunged, grasping for the ball and knocking Julie flat on the floor.

The shrill sound of the ref's whistle stopped the game.

Julie curled up on the court, holding her hand close to her chest in pain. Next thing she knew, she was being helped off the court, and Tracy was at her side.

"Where's Dad?" Julie asked in a shaky voice.

"I don't know," Tracy said. "I haven't seen him. I just got here myself. What happened?"

"Let's have a look at that hand," said Coach Manley. He was already calling for ice and a first-aid kit.

"It's my finger. It bent backward under me when I was pushed down. I can't move it."

"Looks like you have some swelling all right. We'll ice it, and we need to get you to the emergency room for an X-ray," said Coach Manley.

"Leave the game? Please, no!" If she left the game now, people would *really* think that girls shouldn't play basketball. "Coach, can't we tape it up or something so that I can stay in? Can I at least take my free throw?"

"No. I hope it's just a sprain, but I'm not taking any chances," said Coach Manley. "Is your mom or dad here?"

"Just my sister," said Julie.

"Our dad's supposed to be here," said Tracy, "but I don't see him anywhere."

T. J. was standing right next to Julie. "My mom's here. She could take you," he offered. He ran over to the bleachers to alert his mother.

Tracy helped Julie out through the gym door, and the sounds of the clapping, cheering crowd faded as they walked down the empty hall and out the front doors of the school. Clutching her injured finger to her chest, Julie couldn't help thinking that leaving the game hurt almost as much as the pulsing and throbbing of her finger.

Julie sat tense and rigid in a straight-backed chair in the

hospital waiting room. Holding ice to her purple, swollen finger, she fought back tears.

"Can I get you anything, honey?" T. J.'s mother asked, putting her hand on Julie's shoulder.

"Just my mom and dad," Julie sniffed. So much for Cool Hand Albright. How could her hand have let her down like this?

"Tracy's calling them now, and by the time you get done with the doctor, I'm sure they'll be here," said T. J.'s mother.

"You don't understand," said Julie. "My mom and dad don't live together anymore. They're . . . divorced. My dad was supposed to be at the game, and I don't know what happened. Tracy already called Mom twice and can't reach her, either."

"Well, I'll stay with you girls until we reach one of your parents. Don't you worry about that. Right now we just need to get you in to the doctor and feeling better."

Just then, Tracy came back from using the pay phone.

"Any luck?" T. J.'s mother asked her.

"Still no answer," said Tracy. "Mom had to go to a meeting at the bank today. She must not be back yet, and I don't know which bank it is. My dad has a new answering machine, so I left him a message on it. I'll just keep trying."

"Julie Albright," called a nurse, looking down at her clipboard. "Julie Albright."

❀

Julie and Tracy spent nearly an hour behind a curtain at the emergency room while the doctor took X-rays of Julie's finger. Then he listened to her heart, looked into her ears, and shone a bright beam of light in her eyes. By the time she emerged, her arm was resting safely in a sling, and her broken finger was splinted and taped to its neighbor so that she couldn't bend it or move it.

"There she is," a familiar voice exclaimed. Dad! Julie looked up. Rushing down the hall toward her were Mom *and* Dad. Together.

They hurried over to Julie, enfolding her in one big hug. All the tears that she'd been holding back came out in a flood of relief.

"Honey, honey, we just heard. Are you okay?" Mom asked, dabbing tears from Julie's face with the corner of her scarf. "Does it hurt? You girls must have been so scared," she said, looking up at Tracy. "Thank you so much," she added, turning to T. J.'s mother.

"We got here as fast as we could," said Dad, kneeling down to take a closer look at Julie's finger and splint. "What happened? Is anything broken?"

"We were at Julie's basketball game," said Tracy. "This big kid from the other team kept pushing Julie. He wouldn't leave her alone—"

"And they weren't even calling it a foul," added Julie. "Then next thing I knew, he knocked into me, and I fell and landed on my finger. It bent way back the wrong way and hurt really bad and—"

"She broke her finger!" Tracy interrupted, looking back and forth from Mom to Dad.

"Except the doctor kept calling it a *phalange*," said Julie. "Now I'm like a robot," she added, holding up her splinted finger to show off all the metal and gauze around it.

"We'll take care of your finger, and it'll heal soon," Mom reassured her. "I'm just so sorry this happened."

"We're very proud of both of you girls," said Dad. "Tracy, honey, I know this was a lot for you to handle—"

"Where were you, Dad?" Tracy snapped. "You were supposed to be there! What if I hadn't made it to the game after tennis?" Tracy's voice was shaking.

"Tracy," Mom said gently, "your father had a weather delay out of Chicago, and there was nothing he could do. These things happen, and it's nobody's fault. We're all just relieved that Julie's okay."

"I tried to call you a bunch of times," Tracy told Mom.

"I know," said Mom. "It's a good thing Dad got that answering machine. He got your message and called me at the bank, and we came here just as soon as we could. You did the right thing, honey. I know how scary it is when you're worried." Mom pulled Tracy closer, stroking her hair.

"You came with Dad? Together? In the same car?" Julie asked.

"Yes, honey, we did. Dad picked me up on the way." Mom smiled, and Tracy seemed to relax a bit.

A nurse came over and checked Julie's splint one final time. "Looks like you're good to go," she announced.

"Anybody hungry?" asked Dad. "What do you say we head out and stop for pizza?"

"You mean it?" Julie asked. "Can I, Mom?"

"I mean all of us," Dad said. "It's been a rough day for everyone, and I think we could all use a break. How 'bout it?"

"I certainly don't mind not cooking tonight," said Mom.

"And I can't do the dishes anyway!" said Julie, pointing to her sling.

Julie looked over at Tracy, afraid she would refuse Dad's invitation. *Say yes, say yes,* Julie pleaded silently.

"Okay, I guess," said Tracy. "But only if we go to our old place in North Beach, so I can order the Very, Very Veggie pizza."

"Now, Tracy—" Mom started.

"It's okay," said Dad. "I don't mind driving us over there, and then taking you all back to your place. We can

get two pizzas, so you can each choose your favorite. What do you say to that?"

Mom smiled and nodded.

"Wow," said Julie, looking from Mom to Dad. "I should break my finger more often!"

The Best Thing Ever

❀ Chapter 10 ❀

It felt funny to be home resting on the couch on a school day. Mom had told Julie she could stay home since it was Friday and the doctor had recommended taking it easy for a few days.

Mom sat beside her. "Honey, I need to open the shop for at least a few hours today. Will you be okay by yourself for a little while? I'm right downstairs in the shop if you need me. Come on down if you feel up to it."

"I should probably stay and work on my report. It's due on Monday," Julie said. "I have most of it on tape, but I haven't started writing it down yet. Hey, wait a minute—how am I going to write?" Julie held up her splinted finger.

"Hmm, that is a problem," said Mom. "Should I write a note to Ms. Hunter and ask if you can turn it in late?"

"I have a better idea," beamed Julie, jumping up off the sofa. "What if I could turn in my report on tape? I have a lot of it done that way, and I could finish it up without having to write anything."

"Sounds like a creative solution to me," said Mom. "I'll call Ms. Hunter and let her know."

Julie spent the rest of the morning editing her project, erasing certain parts of the tape and adding a few peppy introductions. "Coming up next: the exciting adventures of my dad, daredevil pilot Daniel Albright, when he was my same age. Hold on to your seats!"

Scanning the list of topics for her project, Julie's finger stopped at the Best Thing That Ever Happened to Me. She had planned to tell about the petition and getting onto the boys' basketball team. Momentarily, she was warmed by the memory of last night—being together as a family again, all four of them, the way it used to be. As if nothing had ever changed. Being a family again last night was possibly the Best Thing That Ever Happened. But if she were to include *that* in her report, it meant she would have to mention the Worst Thing.

When it came to the Worst Thing That Ever Happened, it seemed even harder to say the word *divorce* out loud into a tape recorder than to write it down. Julie turned on the tape recorder and pushed the *record* button. She held the microphone up to her face, but no words came.

"The worst thing that ever happened to me," Julie finally stammered, "was when . . ." She couldn't finish her sentence. Giving up, she pressed the *stop* button.

Feeling discouraged, Julie stared at her broken finger. Hey, wait a minute—breaking a finger was a bad thing that had happened to her. Not finishing the biggest basketball game of the season was a bad thing that had happened. Julie didn't even have to say a word about the divorce. Her broken finger could be the Worst Thing That Ever Happened.

Julie turned the tape player back on, pushed the *record* button, and held up the microphone. In a strong voice like a radio announcer, she told the whole story of the Best Thing Ever—the time she collected one hundred fifty signatures on a petition that convinced the principal and school board to let her play on the boys' basketball team. Then, for the Worst Thing Ever, she recounted the game against the Wildcats, complete with her trip to the hospital and her freakish Frankenstein of a finger.

Just as Julie was finishing her recording, Tracy came home from school. She plopped down on the sofa with her tennis racket.

"How was school today? Did you have to turn in your science journal?" Julie asked nervously.

"Yep. And guess what? I got an A. Even though my plant died."

Julie let out a small breath and sank back into the sofa with relief. "Tracy?" she said tentatively. "There's something I have to tell you."

Tracy set down her tennis racket. "What is it?"

"You know that time I watched your plant for you?" said Julie. "Well, I . . . um, I knocked it out the window by mistake. It was an accident, honest! I was afraid you'd be mad at me and flunk your assignment, so I tried to fix it."

"I know," said Tracy.

"You mean you knew all this time?"

Tracy cocked her head. "I figured you broke the pot. Did you really think I wouldn't be able to tell the difference between a hippo and a pig?"

"I guess not," said Julie in a small voice.

"Why didn't you just tell me what happened instead of going to all that trouble to cover it up?"

Julie squirmed and looked down. "I'm sorry," she said finally. "Really, I am. I was going to tell you before you had to turn in your report, but when you were so mad at Dad yesterday for not being at the game and letting you down, I lost my nerve."

For a few moments, Tracy was quiet, and Julie was afraid her sister was angry. But when Tracy spoke, she just sounded sad. "I know I shouldn't have blown up at Dad. It wasn't his fault he wasn't at the game. But sometimes it's hard not to feel as if—well, as if he's let us down in a really big way. By leaving the family, I mean. By getting divorced." Tracy's voice quivered suddenly, and she turned away.

"But they *both* got divorced," Julie pointed out. "It

wasn't just Dad; it was Mom, too. It's not fair to blame the whole thing on Dad."

Tracy was silent. When she turned back to Julie, her eyes were bright, and she blinked a few times to clear them. "You know it's important to tell the truth, Jules." She reached over and tweaked her sister's ponytail. "Besides, we're sisters, and sisters have to stick together. Promise me, next time you'll come talk to me and tell me?"

"Promise," said Julie. She hesitated a moment, then leaned forward and gave Tracy a hug.

On Monday morning, Julie was fumbling and trying to open her locker left-handed when T. J. saw her and called, "Hey, it's Cool Hand Albright. You're back! Let's see the big cast. My mom says you've got mettle, whatever that means."

Julie held up her splint for T. J. to see. "Oh, I've got *metal* all right! Broke my finger. Now I'm the bionic girl."

"Oh, man," said T. J. "I can't believe Dunk ran you over."

"And I can't believe I had to miss the biggest game of the season," said Julie. "Thanks for calling to tell me how the rest of the game went. I'm so bummed out we didn't win."

"But we came super close. Coach said we played our best game ever. We probably would have won if they hadn't injured our star player," T. J. teased.

"Thanks," said Julie with a smile. Taking a deep breath, she grabbed her tape recorder with her left hand, slammed her locker shut, and headed for Ms. Hunter's class, hurrying down the hall side by side with T. J.

Everybody buzzed around Julie, talking about the big game and Julie's broken finger. Like the Telephone game, the story had grown with each telling. One student had heard that Julie was rushed to the hospital in an ambulance. Another had heard that her finger got gangrene and had to be cut off! Julie had not been this popular since the day her mother had visited her class for Career Day and had given everybody free bracelets and mood rings.

Ms. Hunter clapped her hands, and the students returned to their seats to listen to one another's reports.

Angela went first. For the Worst Thing That Ever Happened, she told about the time she jumped into the pool and her bathing suit bottom came off. The whole class burst out laughing, and Ms. Hunter had to blink the lights to get everybody to settle down.

T. J. went next. He called his report "Cheaper by the Half Dozen" and told about living with five sisters. (Julie couldn't imagine having five sisters—one was plenty.) T. J. described how his mom gave all the kids haircuts to save money. For the girls, she just trimmed a few inches off the ends, but for T. J., she put a bowl on top of his head and cut off all the hair below it. T. J. showed a picture of himself in second grade, looking like Moe from the Three Stooges.

"Now who's brave," Julie whispered when T. J. sat down. "That took super-duper courage to show everybody that picture!"

Finally, it was Julie's turn. Carrying her tape recorder, she walked to the front of the class. "As everybody knows, I broke my finger on my right hand, so I couldn't write out my report in handwriting," she started to explain.

"Aw, let's have a pity party," one of the students said.

"Hey, my finger hurts too," somebody else called out.

Julie laughed. "For real, I had to record my report on tape. So I'm going to play it for you now."

The class listened intently to the stories of jumping on her parents' bed, Dad's big bike ride, Mom's runaway horse, and the Best Thing Ever—the petition and playing basketball for the Jaguars. Finally, Julie's voice on the tape said, "And last but not least, I'm going to tell you about the Worst Thing That Ever Happened to Me."

Click. Julie turned off the tape recorder.

"Hey, no fair!" said a boy in the back row. "You have to let us hear the worst thing. That's the best part!"

Julie looked hesitantly at her teacher. Her palms were beginning to sweat, yet her throat felt as dry as chalk dust. "Ms. Hunter," she said, trying to swallow, "would it be okay if I just tell the last part aloud, I mean, without the tape? I sort of changed my mind about what I want to say."

"I don't see that as a problem," said Ms. Hunter.

Julie straightened her slumped shoulders and began. "I was going to play back the story of my broken finger for the Worst Thing That Ever Happened to Me," she explained. "But really, that wouldn't be telling the truth. Because even worse than a broken finger is when my family broke apart. A few months ago, my mom and dad got a divorce. That means I don't live with both of my parents anymore."

Julie's stomach turned somersaults. She wanted to go get a drink of water, but she forced her feet to stand steady.

"When I broke my finger," she continued, "my mom and dad both came to the hospital. And after I got bandaged up, we all went out for pizza together. I was so happy to have us all back together again that it was almost worth breaking my finger. Except that it only lasted for one night. We weren't together again for real, permanently." Julie paused, thinking what to say next. This time the class was dead quiet, waiting for her to continue.

Julie knew she had covered all the topics for her report, but she realized there was still something she was trying to say. "Just now, as I was playing back the tape, I remembered something my dad told me when he broke his foot. He said that a broken bone heals back together even stronger than before it was broken."

Julie's stomach was feeling less queasy, and her voice was stronger now, more confident. "I think families are kind of like bones—they can break too, but in some ways, it makes you even stronger. And when one person's in trouble or gets hurt, families pull together, and you can still count on them to be there for you.

"The end. That's the Story of My Life. So far."

Everybody clapped. Julie walked down the aisle, her heart still pounding. She slid into her chair, aware now of the pulsing in her injured finger. She knew in her heart that the break in her family would always be there. But the love she felt for her sister and her parents, and the love they felt for her, was as strong as ever. That part couldn't be broken.

When Julie was growing up, many people didn't think girls could do the same things boys did. They thought only boys should become doctors or lawyers or scientists or athletes. They thought sports, especially team sports like basketball, should be only for boys. Some schools didn't even have gym classes for girls.

But these views were beginning to change. Some leaders in Congress wanted girls to have the same opportunities boys had at school, so they passed a law in 1972 making sex discrimination illegal for any school that received money

Katy Steding, left, was the only girl on her youth league basketball team. She went on to play for one of the first women's professional teams, the Portland Power. That's Katy holding the ball at right.

from the federal government—which included nearly every school in the country, from elementary to college. This law became known as Title Nine (often written Title IX).

At first, schools didn't realize how many changes Title Nine would require. But soon they realized that the new law meant they had to provide athletic teams for girls—or else let girls play on the boys' teams. One ten-year-old girl named Dot Richardson loved baseball but had no team to play on. So she helped her brother warm up for his Little League games by pitching balls to him. When the coach saw how well Dot pitched, he invited her to play. Since Little League didn't allow girls, he told her, "We're going to have to cut your hair short and give you a boy's name." But Dot didn't want to pretend she was a boy! After Title Nine, she joined a girls' fast-pitch softball team and became one of the best players in the country.

Jackie Adams was one of the first girls to play with boys on a Little League baseball team.

Dot Richardson went on to win a gold medal in softball at the 1996 Olympics. She later became a surgeon.

In Julie's day, tennis was one of the few sports with professional women players, but compared with the male players they received little pay or respect. Tennis pro Bobby Riggs claimed that a man could beat any woman on the court. In 1973 he challenged tennis pro Billie Jean King to a well-publicized match known as the "Battle of the Sexes." Because Bobby Riggs had proudly called himself a "male chauvinist pig," Billie Jean King gave him a baby pig as a gift before the game started!

Billie Jean King

Billie Jean prepared hard for the match. She knew that if she lost, it would confirm what a lot of people thought: that females shouldn't be taken seriously as athletes. She creamed Bobby Riggs in three straight sets, sending a powerful message that female athletes could play just as well as men.

Sports wasn't the only arena in which attitudes about girls and women were changing. Before Julie's time, most jobs for women were limited to nursing, teaching, or service jobs like waitress or cashier. These jobs did not pay as well as men's jobs. But by the 1970s, girls were going on to college and graduate school in record numbers. As more colleges and professional schools admitted women, thanks to Title Nine, more and more women became lawyers, doctors, businesswomen, and scientists—jobs that

Sally Ride studied physics to become America's first woman astronaut.

traditionally had been held by men. Many women simply wanted the satisfaction of doing respected, well-paid work. Others worked because they had to. In many families like Julie's, where the parents had divorced, women had to go out and earn an income, often for the first time.

Before the 1970s, divorce was rare. Since women had limited opportunities for work outside the home, leaving a marriage often meant financial hardship. Besides, as Julie knew, getting divorced carried *stigma*, or a strong sense of public shame. Parents usually felt it was best for their children if they stayed together, even when their marriage wasn't happy. But by the mid-1970s, women had more options. Many went back to school or started a business, so they were no longer dependent on their husbands for income. When a couple found they had different ideas about how to live their lives, they sometimes chose to get divorced.

More and more women—including those who stayed happily married—started seeing themselves as independent

Gloria Steinem cofounded Ms. *magazine, which focused on women's new roles and options.*

people with ideas and skills of their own. To make this point, some women stopped identifying themselves in the traditional way by their husband's name, such as "Mrs. John Smith." Instead, they adopted the title Ms., followed

People outside the White House, reading the news of President Nixon's resignation

by their own name, "Ms. Susan Smith," whether they were married or single, just as Julie's teacher did.

These social changes weren't easy. Americans were reeling from other major changes. They recently had watched President Richard Nixon resign over the scandal known as Watergate. Shocked that their president had tried to cover up the burglary of files from his political opponents and then had lied to the public about it, many Americans lost confidence in

their government. The public was also deeply divided over the Vietnam War. Protestors filled the streets, and by the early 1970s, a majority of people disapproved of the war. It sometimes seemed as if all the time-honored American ideals were being turned upside down.

For Americans who wanted their world to stay the same, such profound changes—in their government, their jobs, their marriages, and even their sports—were upsetting. But other Americans, especially young people, welcomed the changes. They believed that creating a fairer society, where girls and women had the same opportunities as boys and men, would improve life for all Americans.

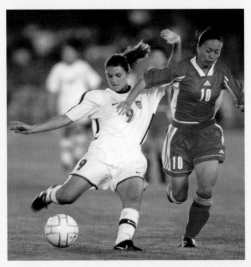

Title Nine created opportunities for talented players like soccer star Mia Hamm, whose team won the Women's World Cup in 1999.

At midday the wagon train stopped in a field where the horses could graze. Julie and April liked to wander among the wagons, saying hello to the other people, and each trying to be the first to spot Jimmy and Hurricane. One day they found Jimmy hunched over his saddle, fixing a stirrup strap. Hurricane was tied to a nearby tree.

Jimmy looked up as the girls approached. "April, would you take Hurricane down to the stream for a drink?"

April nodded. She untied Hurricane's rope and started across the field toward the creek. Suddenly she turned to Julie. "Hey, want to ride Hurricane? I'll boost you up."

"Really?" Julie's heart began to pound. "But wait. What about a saddle?"

"You can ride bareback," said April. "It's super fun. C'mon, I'll give you a leg up." She cupped her hands to

make a foothold. Julie stepped into April's hand and, in one swift motion, swung her other leg up and over the horse. "Hold on to his mane," April instructed.

As April led Hurricane across the grassy field, Julie wobbled from side to side. Hurricane's bare back was slippery. She hunkered down low, clinging to the horse's mane.

"Try to relax," April coached. "Sit up straight and get your balance."

Gradually Julie sat up a little taller, gripping the sides of the horse with her thighs. She eased into the rocking motion of the horse, feeling his warmth against her legs, his back muscles rippling with each step.

"Good—that's it. You're getting it," said April.

"I'm really riding!" said Julie.

"You're doing great! Want to try a trot?" April asked.

"Sure, why not," said Julie.

"Here, take the rope." April tossed the end of the lead rope up to her. Julie let go of the mane with one hand and caught it.

"Now kick him with your heels," April called. She broke into a jog. "Let's go, Hurricane."

Julie swung out her feet and gave the horse a kick. Hurricane shot across the field, heading straight for the creek. *Ba-da-rump, ba-da-rump, ba-da-rump.* All Julie could hear was the beating of hooves and the whoosh of air in her ears. "Help!" she called, but April was already far behind.

"*Hangggg onnn!*" April's voice was nearly lost in the thundering of hooves.

Julie clung desperately to Hurricane's side, one leg barely hooked over his back. She clutched at his mane. All she could see was the ground—and Hurricane's pounding hooves. Dust stung her eyes. Her heart thumped against her rib cage. If she fell, surely she'd be trampled.

Just when Julie thought she couldn't hang on another second, Hurricane came to a dead stop at the creek's edge. Julie didn't remember letting go. She didn't remember flying through the air. All she knew was the smack of cold water and the bite of a large rock under her shoulder. The wind was knocked out of her. She took in a ragged breath and scrambled backward on all fours to get away from Hurricane, who was calmly taking a drink.

"Julie, are you okay?" April asked, helping her to her feet. "Oh no, you're sopping wet. You look like a drowned rat!" She began to giggle.

"It's not funny," said Julie. "I almost got trampled. And after I fell, I could hardly even breathe."

April picked up the lead rope. "You'll be okay. Falling is part of learning to ride. You have to fall at least seven times before you're a good rider."

"Well, forget about learning to ride, then," Julie muttered. "I'm not getting back up on that horse."

"Oh, don't be such a baby. Look, I won't let go of the rope this time, and we'll just stay at a walk."

"I'm not a baby," said Julie, but her voice came out all wobbly and her legs felt like spaghetti. The girls headed back across the field in silence.

"Hey, Julie, just think—this is kind of like the time in *Little House on the Prairie* when Nellie fell off Laura's horse," said April.

Julie glowered at her cousin. "For your information," she snapped, "that was just in the TV show. The *real* Laura never took Nellie riding—she took her into the stream so that Nellie would get leeches on her legs."

"Leeches? Eeww!" April began to giggle. But this time it didn't make Julie laugh.

After lunch, she wrote in her diary,

I don't care what April or anybody says. I'm not getting back on that horse—ever.

Reading about pioneers is not the same as doing it. Maybe it wasn't so hard for Laura when she sat bareback on one of Pa's plow horses, but Hurricane is no plow horse, that's for sure.

I never would have made it as a pioneer. Why did I even come on this trip?